Buried Treasures of the Appalachians

Buried Treasures of the Appalachians

Legends of Homestead Caches, Indian Mines and Loot from Civil War Raids

W.C. Jameson

August House Publishers, Inc.

L I T T L E   R O C K

Published by August House, Inc.,
P.O. Box 3223, Little Rock, Arkansas, 72203,
501-372-5450.

Printed in the United States of America

10 9 8 7 6 5 4 3 2 1

LIBRARY OF CONGRESS CATALOGING-IN-PUBLICATION DATA

Jameson, W. C., 1942-
Buried Treasures of the Appalachians : legends of homestead caches, Indian mines, and loot from Civil War raids / W. C. Jameson — 1st ed.
p. cm.
Includes bibliographical references.

ISBN 0-87483-126-1 (acid-free) : $9.95
1. Treasure-trove—Appalachian Mountains—Folklore. 1. Tales—Appalachian Mountains. I. Title.
GR108.J36 1991
398.27'0974—dc20 91-3453

First Edition, 1991

Executive: Liz Parkhurst
Project editor: Judith Faust
Design director: Ted Parkhurst
Cover design: Wendell E. Hall
Typography: Lettergraphics, Little Rock

This book is printed on archival-quality paper which meets the guidelines for performance and durability of the Committee on Production Guidelines for Book Longevity of the Council on Library Resources.

AUGUST HOUSE, INC. PUBLISHERS LITTLE ROCK

For my son
Luke

Contents

Prologue

For many years I have searched for, researched, and collected tales of buried treasures and lost mines associated with the Appalachian Mountains. The Appalachians have always been one of my favorite places, and when the time came to put some stories together in a book, I decided to go there again for a while to get reacquainted with the land and the people I have come to respect and admire.

On this trip, I wanted to avoid the big cities and concentrate on the rural areas and the remote settlements where a way of life common to several generations past is still led by many of the residents.

As I drove through isolated valleys and hollows and across lonesome ridgetops, I found it hard to believe the gentle rolling landscape of the Appalachian Mountains was the product of violent upheaval of the earth's crust accompanied by massive folding, faulting, and volcanic activity millions of years ago. As I inhaled the sweet aroma of the green fields and watched dazzling displays of butterflies coloring the landscape, I was struck again with the odd truth that this range of mountains, once higher than the Rockies, that had been a place of bloodshed in the French and Indian War and the War Between The States, that had seen poverty and suffering, prosperity and progress, contains some of the most serene, tranquil, and placid environments on the continent. During their life of well over two hundred million years, the Appalachian Mountains have mellowed into a comfortable, peaceful haven that is a balm for the spirit, an elixir for the soul.

Reminders of the eons-old processes that created this range were apparent along many of the roads I traveled: layered outcrops of highly fractured and weathered limestone; seams of coal, which have sometimes supported the area's economy; occasional outcrops of granite, suggestive of the igneous forces deep below the crust that formed rich veins of gold and silver.

The people I encountered here were as much a part of the landscape as the rocks and trees. Salt-of-the-earth types they were, and their creased features reminded me of the worn limestone on which they walked. I saw few young people in these remote settings; most of those I met were old-timers, and they were often wary of strangers—retiring, almost secretive, and very territorial.

The few I managed to coax into conversation spoke a dialect I have been told can be traced to Elizabethan England, and many had decidedly old English surnames like Yadkin, Cabot, Calloway, and Williams. Here and there, one could detect the presence of Indian blood among them, an element that lent further mystery to their mien.

Many were reluctant to talk to me at first, but when my intentions became clear, they opened up. At first they were cautious, but before long, they were open and free in conversations as if they craved the opportunity to tell newcomers of the wonders of their valleys and mountains. They told of living off the land, of poaching game and gathering ginseng, of whiskey stills. They told me about folk treatments for ailments such as cancer and arthritis, and how they seldom visited physicians and hospitals. And they told many stories of lost mines and buried treasures.

I had heard a number of the stories before, but the native versions were always a little different, perhaps a bit more personal. Many others were completely new to me. The captivating tales were about the rich mines and buried ingots of gold and silver of the Spanish explorers who came there centuries ago, about Indian silver in abundance, about the mining activities of the first settlers, about Civil

War loot—about fortunes made and cached and forgotten and lost. They told of the ongoing search for many of these treasures and of clinging to the belief that the tales are true and that it is only a matter time until someone chances upon a lost fortune.

These stories are a strong and important component of the culture of these mountain folk. Long tucked away in the isolated recesses of the mountains, their ways of life and their folktales remained elusive, almost unknown, for generations. Now the people and their stories are the object of study and analysis at major universities throughout the country—folklorists from as far away as Europe are arriving in the Appalachians regularly to record the ways of these mountain people.

Returning to my home and manuscript, I reread many of the stories I intended to include in this book. It occurred to me that some of them lacked two essential ingredients—the flavor of the Appalachian people and the strong sense of place one feels when in these mountains. Using what I learned from the folk, I rewrote many of the stories and added bits of color and information gleaned from my visit with the mountain people.

These stories belong to them.

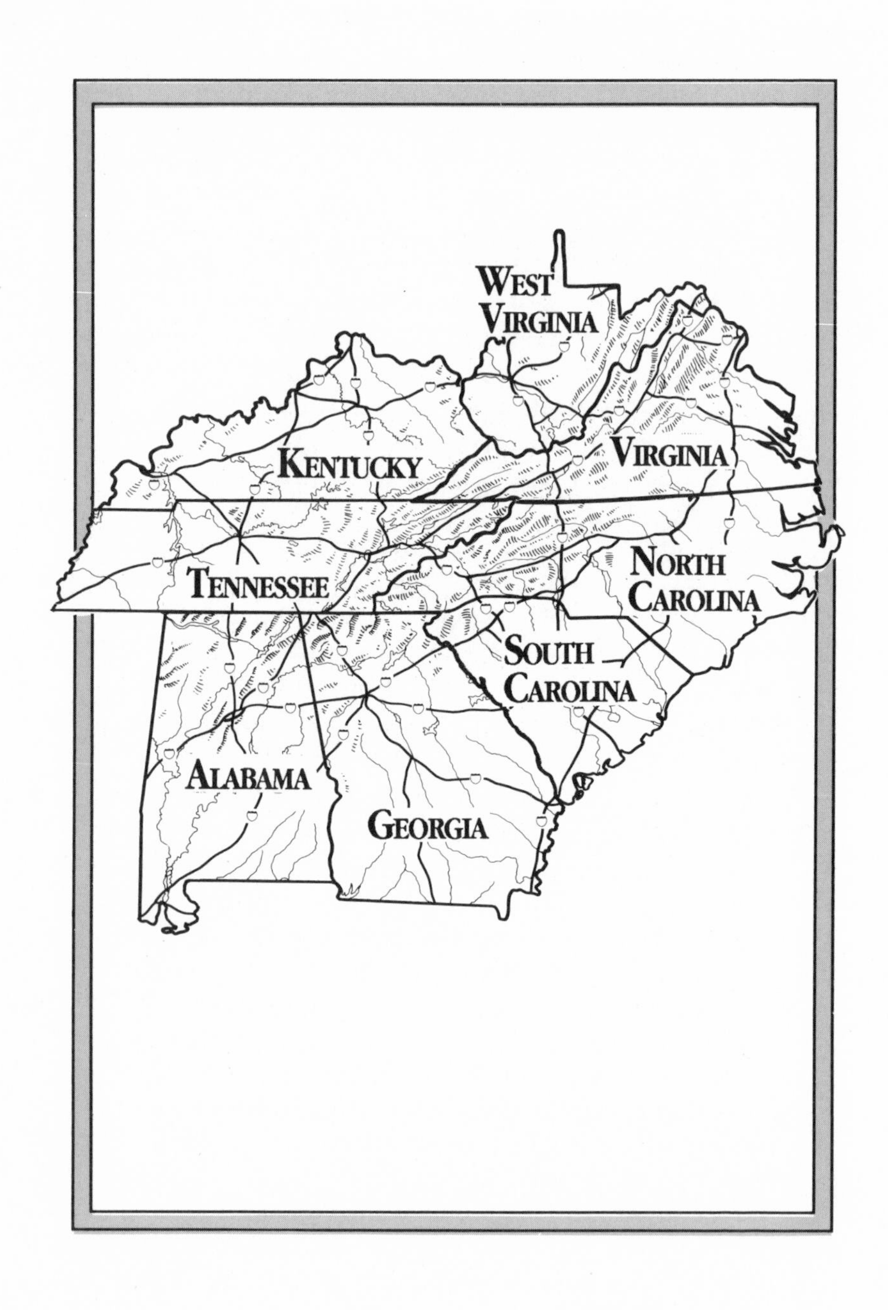
WEST VIRGINIA
KENTUCKY
VIRGINIA
TENNESSEE
NORTH CAROLINA
SOUTH CAROLINA
ALABAMA
GEORGIA

Introduction

Of all the major mountain ranges in North America, none possesses more enduring images than the Appalachians. Our sterotypes are strong: many of us see the Appalachian Mountains as rugged and remote, a setting for feuding and moonshining, populated by religious fundamentalists and backward hillbillies resisting every encroachment of civilization. We also think of the Appalachians as rich in the tradition of oral history and folklore, and rife with wonderful tales of long ago. Prominent among them are colorful legends of lost and buried treasures.

Because modern Appalachia is much like any other settled portion of the United States, perceptions of backwardness are largely unfair and inaccurate, though, to be sure, there are people living in remote sections of these mountains whose activities, priorities, and social structures differ little from those of a hundred years ago. Today, however, the Appalachian range has been transected by interstates and railroads, accommodates several major universities, medical centers, and industrial and corporate complexes, and claims among its cities some of the most progressive urban areas in the country.

The Appalachian Mountains have fascinated Americans, and the range played a significant role in the early settlement of the United States. Within the geographic realm of the Appalachian Mountains wars have been fought, fortunes made and lost, some unique cultures spawned and others forced into extinction.

The Appalachian Mountains are a complex region, both environmentally and culturally. They are home to a great diversity of natural settings and people, and within their borders can be found a variety and abundance of natural resources, recreational opportunities, wildlife habitats, and climates.

Origins

The Appalachian Mountains spread across fourteen states and comprise a major physiographic component of the nation east of the Mississippi River. The range is considerably older than the Rocky Mountains in the west, having matured over the past 225,000,000 years into a stable, tectonically inactive range manifesting comparatively little faulting and no active folding or volcanism, although these processes were very common early in the evolution of the mountains.

The Appalachian Mountains separate the coastal plain of the eastern seaboard from the extensive plains bordering the valleys of the Ohio and Mississippi Rivers to the west. The Appalachians are physiographically characterized as a combination of highly folded regions and extensive plateaus that separate the central part of the range from the Atlantic coastal plain to the east and the interior lowlands to the west. Millions of years of erosion, primarily from rivers and streams, have reduced the once towering Appalachians to a series of gently rounded and smoothly sculpted low-lying mountains. The relatively soft sedimentary rocks which make up much of the plateau provinces have been worn into deep valleys creating significant relief between the uplands and lowlands.

The Appalachians had their origins well over two hundred twenty-five million years ago. Around this time, called the Paleozoic Era, the region of North America that was to become the Appalachian Mountains was a Mediterranean-type sea. For millions of years, sediments from the adjacent lands washed into this sea, building to a thickness of thousands of feet, and above these sediments lay the weight of the shallow sea. As the sediments accumulated and increased in thickness and weight, they caused the underlying crust to sink, thus creating a huge trough called a geosyncline which deepened at a rate of about one foot every ten thousand years.

Near the end of the Paleozoic Era, the sinking and resulting trough-development movements were reversed—the now lithified sediments in the huge geosyncline were folded and uplifted as a result of compressional stresses from repeated long-term collision of two great continental plates. As the plates collided, one overrode the other, resulting in intense fracturing and folding accompanied by occasional volcanism. This occurred at least three times during the period, and the result was the gradual elevation of a vast area that became the Appalachian Mountains.

During the folding and fracturing of this part of the earth's surface, molten material from deep below the crust intruded into zones of fracture and weakness. As the pressurized magma worked its way up through the crust, it traveled far from its heat source and, lacking sufficient pressure to break through to the surface, cooled underground over successive centuries, eventually producing vast formations of granite threaded with rich seams of gold and silver.

Once the Appalachians were uplifted to significant altitudes, the mountains were exposed to highly efficient erosion by flowing water, glaciation, and wind. As a result, much of the granite and other igneous rocks with their veins of gold and silver were exposed at the surface. The weathered rock debris resulting from erosion was carried downslope toward the Atlantic Ocean, burying the volcanic and metamorphic roots of these Paleozoic mountains in sediments reaching hundreds of feet thick.

The varying intensities of the folding and faulting processes caused such significant differences in topography throughout this vast and unique geographic area that scientists have classified the range into four distinct subdivisions, or provinces: the Piedmont Plateau, the Blue Ridge, the Valley and Ridge, and the Appalachian Plateau.

The Piedmont Plateau, which provides a transition from the higher elevations of the range to the Atlantic Coastal Plains of Maryland, Virginia, the Carolinas, and Georgia, is composed primarily of gneiss, schist, marble, quartzite, and slate, all metamorphic rocks formed from the intense heat and pressures of earlier geologic eras.

The Blue Ridge province, following the general direction of the Appalachians, runs approximately southwest-to-northeast and varies in width from five to fifty miles. The mountains here generally rise from one to five thousand feet above the Appalachian Plateau, reaching 6,684 feet at Mount Mitchell in North Carolina. The Blue Ridge is composed primarily of granite and gneiss, with some sedimentary formations, mostly sandstone, siltstone, and conglomerate. The Blue Ridge, while exhibiting some folding, was subjected to intensive faulting and fracturing during the Paleozoic Era.

The Valley and Ridge Province of the Appalachians varies from twenty-five to seventy-five miles wide, is highly faulted, and also displays some impressive folding. Sandstone, shale, and limestone are the most common sedimentary rocks in the region, with the limestone providing ideal conditions for the formation of the numerous impressive and extensive cavern systems found throughout the province.

The Appalachian Plateau, separating the higher elevations of the interior from the riverine lowlands to the immediate west, range from one to three thousand feet in altitude and are composed primarily of highly dissected sedimentary rock. The dissections have created impressively deep valleys throughout much of the region.

As these once lofty mountains eroded, the weathered products of the igneous, metamorphic, and sedimentary rocks contributed to the wide variety of soils found throughout the region. On the sloping hillsides, the soil layers remained somewhat thin but sufficient to support stands of hardwoods and softwoods. In the bottomlands between the ridges, thicker, richer soils accumulated that would later attract farmers and other settlers.

Cultural Environment

The history and culture of Appalachia are at least as significant as its physical setting is beautiful.

Though there are some major urban centers, much of the Appalachian Mountains today remains a world apart, its inhabitants leading lives distant from some of the standards and concepts familiar to other North Americans. This relative isolation, though commonly believed to be widespread, occurs in remote and often widely separated pockets throughout the region. Within these pockets of remnant cultures, a few people live much as their forbears did a hundred or more years ago.

The Appalachians were long avoided by whites. They were seen as a significant barrier to settlement and westward migration—travel into, across, and through the rugged wilderness was often difficult, fraught with hazards such as hostile Indians, rough passage, and flooded rivers. Even so, people continued to come—in search of land, of freedom, of wealth.

The first Appalachian settlers were, of course, the native Americans. These early inhabitants were primarily hunters, gatherers, and fishermen, but some also practiced comparatively sophisticated agriculture, cultivating corn, tobacco, squash, and beans.

Little is known about the Indian occupation of much of the northern Appalachians, but the historical record of Cherokee habitation in the south is quite thorough. In addition to being efficient hunters and farmers, the Cherokee knew how to extract precious-metal ores from the stone matrix of the surrounding hills, and probably learned some new techniques from the early Spanish explorers. With the refining of gold and silver, the Cherokee and neighboring tribes became noted for their skill in fashioning fine jewelry and ornaments. The Indians were also known to store large quantities of the valuable ore.

In the early sixteenth century, the Spanish arrived in the Appalachian Mountains. Soldiers, miners, priests, and explorers under the leadership of Hernando de Soto journeyed to the New World under orders of the Spanish king to secure lands and search for wealth, wealth that was to be taken by whatever means and returned to the motherland to fill the depleted treasury.

The Spaniards came to Appalachia and on several occasions located gold and silver in the rocks of the great mountains. More often than not, de Soto's men merely took over mines that had been worked by the area Indians, but history records that the Spanish experienced amazing success at extracting the ore, smelting it into easily transportable ingots, and shipping it back to Spain.

Generations later, other whites entered the area. Lured by abundant game, a few hardy trappers and hunters journeyed to the Appalachians and returned to the eastern colonies with tales of natural bounty. In their wake came a few of the more adventurous eastern colonists. Initially, the plateau provinces on the edge of the range attracted the newcomers—the best soils were located there, and agriclture was most promising.

As whites gradually moved into the area in pursuit of hunting, trapping, and agricultural opportunities, the Indians were initially very friendly and often served as benefactors to the newcomers, bringing them offerings of their harvests from the fields and forests. Many of the early settlers married into the tribes and acquired Indian land.

After the French and Indian War of the 1750s and 1760s, the British government moved to consolidate control over the Appalachian region. Once the Indian threat was reduced, more and more whites were encouraged to settle in the region. Revolutionary War and French and Indian War veterans were given land grants, the size of the allocation depending on rank and length of service. In addition to veterans with land grants, many squatters found their way onto the rapidly growing plantations and farms.

With the increase in white population, the relationship between the newcomers and the Indian residents grew antagonistic as hunting pressure and competition for land developed. The Indians, regarded until then as friends and allies, were portrayed as ruthless savages bent on destroying white settlers. Tensions grew, conflicts resulted, and the situation grew more strained year by year.

As if all these pressures were not bad enough, about the same time, in the 1760s, gold was discovered in the southern Appalachians, and many intent on getting rich off the newly opened ore fields migrated into the range. As the numbers of white settlers, miners, and soldiers increased, the few Indians that remained were eventually forced off their tribal homelands.

Meanwhile, European newcomers to the colonies were finding conditions considerably more crowded than they had anticipated. The abundant lands and opportunities they believed awaited them in the New World didn't seem to be where they were, so they sought them in the Appalachians, just a few days travel to the west.

The population of whites in the Appalachians continued to grow. Early settlers in the region were primarily English, and these were followed by large numbers of Germans and Scotch-Irish. In lesser numbers came French Huguenots, the Swiss, and other northern Europeans.

The Germans and Scotch–Irish quickly established some of the more extensive farmsteads on the rich alluvial bottomlands, and around these growing and prospering farms, settlements evolved, churches were constructed, and towns began to grow.

Blacks were brought from the deep South to the southern Piedmont to work on cotton and tobacco plantations. Though some blacks worked in the coal mines, only a few ventured into the interior of the Blue Ridge and the Valley and Ridge provinces, and many abandoned the

Appalachian region altogether during and after World War II for job opportunies in the industrial north.

During the 1860s, the Appalachians, as well as other parts of the country, were torn by the War Between The States. Life was disrupted, settlements and farms abandoned, mines closed down, and businesses left in ruins. During the War, millions of dollars in gold and silver payrolls and money for arms, ammunition, and equipment moved through the area. Much of it was stolen, hidden, hoarded, or lost.

The post–War period saw the Appalachian countryside filled with desperate men and outlaws. Banditry was common, and travelers moved through the area at great risk to their lives. After this relatively brief period of outlawry, the area evolved into relative peace and renewed growth and prosperity.

Today the Appalachian Mountains are home to an eclectic cultural mix of various races and ethnic groups, each bringing its part over the years to the diversity, uniqueness, and progress of the region. Every one of the cultures has influenced the region's "personality," contributing to its economy, its educational system, its cultural heritage, and its folklore.

Buried Treasure in the Appalachians

There is much Appalachian folklore that concerns lost and buried treasures, some tales derived from the legacies of the native Americans, others from those of Spanish conquistadors, early white settlers, and the War Between The States. The folklore is distinctly Appalachian, and the tales are replete with colorful narratives of the place, the people, the times, and the age-old quest for wealth and buried treasures.

The lure of lost treasure is a powerful one, and hundreds of Appalachian residents as well as travelers to the area have succumbed to it during past generations. Hard times in the Appalachians caused many mines to close, farms to be abandoned, and people to leave, but the search for buried treasure went on unabated, perhaps even stronger. Some communities in Appalachia did not survive, but the stories did, and like the ancient mountains themselves, they endured.

ALABAMA & GEORGIA

ALABAMA

1. The Treasure of Red Bone Cave
2. Grain Miller's Buried Wealth
3. Lost Silver Mine of the Cherokee
4. Flint River Cherokee Gold
5. Yuchi Gold of Paint Rock Valley

GEORGIA

6. The Secret Treasure Tunnel of the Georgia Cherokee
7. The Lost Treasure of the Red Bank Cherokee
8. The Wandering Confederate Treasury
9. Cohutta Montain Gold
10. Lost Slave Gold Vein

The Treasure of Red Bone Cave

Somewhere on the north side of the Tennessee River near Muscle Shoals is an elusive limestone cavern which may contain several million dollars' worth of gold ingots and jewelry. This treasure cave has been known of for centuries, but efforts to locate it during the past two hundred fifty years have not succeeded.

Legend attributes the origin of the gold to Spanish explorers who came to this region under the leadership of Hernando de Soto. In 1538, Charles V of Spain gave de Soto ample funding and a company of more than six hundred men to travel to the New World to search for silver and gold. The ore was to be smelted, cast into ingots, and shipped to the motherland, Spain.

Arriving in Florida after months crossing the Atlantic Ocean, de Soto and his company of soldiers, miners, and priests traveled, explored, and prospected vast portions of the southern United States from the east coast to the Ozark Mountains. According to ancient records and documents found in Spanish monasteries, the explorers were successful, for they eventually shipped hundreds of millions of dollars' worth of gold and silver back to the Iberian peninsula.

As well as mining for it, de Soto's men took great quantities of gold from several of the Cherokee villages they encountered in their explorations. Though the

Cherokee did not measure wealth with gold, they used the metal to fashion bracelets and other jewelry. When the Spanish saw the abundance of gold the Indians possessed, they took it by force, often killing hundreds of the red men in the process. The jewelry was melted down and formed into brick-sized ingots.

A Spanish detachment that had just raided several Cherokee villages was leading a gold-laden pack train of some forty horses when it chanced upon a friendly Chickasaw encampment in what is now northeastern Alabama. The settlement was a few miles south of the Tennessee River along a tributary that provided good water for drinking and crops.

As winter was coming, the Chickasaw invited the newcomers to remain in their village until the cold weather passed. The Spaniards accepted the invitation and lived for a time with the Indians, joining in their hunts for game.

When spring finally came, the Spaniards began preparing to travel to the southwest to rendezvous with de Soto at a location designated earlier. Before their departure, however, the leader of the party demanded of the Chickasaw chief some one hundred of the tribe's young women to accompany the soldiers on their journey. When the chief refused, the Spaniards became belligerent and threatening.

While they were loading their gold on the pack horses, the Spaniards were surprised by a sudden attack from the enraged Chickasaw. Panicked, the soldiers hastily mounted their horses and fled from the village, leaving behind the great treasure in gold ingots.

The Chickasaw pursued the Spaniards northward to the bank of the Tennessee River. With their retreat cut off, the soldiers turned and fought. The battle lasted nearly an hour, and when it was over, most of the Spaniards had been killed.

After returning to the village, the Chickasaw chief ordered all the treasure carried to a cave across the wide river to the north and concealed within it.

This done, the Indians ignored the great fortune in gold cached in the limestone cavern except when some small amount was needed to make jewelry and ornaments.

The Chickasaw village thrived over the ensuing years, and it was a large and happy community that greeted a young white trapper who entered the region in 1720 in search of beaver. The trapper wanted to try his luck along some of the small streams found in the area. He came to the Chickasaw village and requested permission from the chief to set his traps in the nearby streams.

The Chickasaw chief, impressed by the young man, granted permission and invited him to live in the village. He did so, and during the following weeks, the chief became very fond of the trapper.

The chief had only one child, a daughter, and as he was very old, he was concerned that she find a husband and provide him with a grandson who would eventually lead the tribe. The daughter had spurned the courtship of the many Chickasaw braves, and the chief was beginning to wonder if she would ever wed. The daughter did, however, find the young trapper to her liking, and soon the two of them were spending time together.

One night, about two months after he first entered the Chickasaw village, the trapper was awakened by two Indians. Without a word, they tied his hands behind his back and placed a blindfold over his eyes before he could identify them. He fought as hard as he could, but their combined strength was too much for him. Once he realized he was helpless, he ceased to struggle, and the Indians whispered that no harm would come to him if he followed their instruction.

All the rest of that night and the morning of the following day, the trapper was led through the woods. Once while the group was stopped to rest, the blindfold slipped slightly from the captive's eyes, and he momentarily saw before him the wide expanse of the Tennessee River and the high limestone bluffs that rose in the distance beyond.

A few moments later, he was placed in a canoe and rowed across the river. After a brief hike, the three men came to a place where the air was cold and the ground was damp. The trapper could hear the squeaks of bats and realized he was inside a large cave.

Fifteen minutes further into the cave, the Indians called a halt, untied the trapper, and removed the blindfold.

The three men stood in a large chamber illuminated by torches. As the light flickered on the walls of the cave, the trapper looked around and recognized the chief of the Chickasaw village and one of his braves. The chief directed the trapper's eyes to one of the walls of the cave.

Stacked like cordwood against the far wall of the chamber were hundreds of ingots of pure gold, reaching nearly to the ceiling. At the foot of the stack were several chests filled with golden jewels and other valuables.

The chief told the trapper the tale of the long-ago Spaniards' visit. The chief also told him that the gold he saw in this room was only a part of the total amount hidden in the cave.

Taking the trapper to another chamber in the cave, the chief pointed to several skeletons propped against one wall. He said they were the bones of the warriors that had died in the battle with the fleeing Spaniards. The bodies were placed in the cave so their spirits could guard it against intruders.

The chief came forward and laid a hand on the trapper's shoulder. He told the young man that if he married his daughter, all the treasure in the other room would be his to keep. If he chose not to marry the daughter, he would be allowed to leave the village unharmed but was not to know the location of the treasure cave.

The trapper considered his options. If he married the chief's daughter and remained in the remote Indian village, the wealth would do him little good, as he would have no opportunity to spend it. Remembering his view of the river and the limestone bluff when the blindfold slipped from his eyes earlier that day, he believed he would be able to return and locate the cave on his own.

The trapper told the Chickasaw chief he wanted a few days alone to consider the offer. The chief agreed, reattached the bindings and the blindfold, and led the trapper from the cave.

Darkness fell long before the party could reach the village, and as they were all tired, the chief decided to camp for the night near the bank of the river. Late that night, the trapper killed the two Indians while they slept and threw their bodies into the river. He then fled on foot to Fort Rosalie in the Natchez Territory, reaching it after a harrowing journey of several days.

At the fort, the trapper invited an old friend to join him in his search for the great treasure of what he called Red Bone Cave, naming it after the skeletons of the red men he saw within it.

Hiding by day and searching by night, the two men spent the next several weeks trying to find the cave. The trapper's friend grew weary of the fruitless search and soon returned to Fort Rosalie.

Now alone, the trapper decided to return to the Chickasaw village. Wary at first, he was surprised when he was warmly welcomed by the Indians. He learned later that no one had ever known that the chief and his accomplice had kidnapped him and taken him from the village that night a few months earlier. The disappearance of the chief and the brave remained a mystery to the Indians.

Using the excuse of trapping for furs, the young man continued his search for Red Bone Cave. He eventually married the daughter of the dead chief and settled in the village, and though he searched for many years, he was never able to find the cave again.

In 1723, the trapper's wife died from malaria, and he eventually returned to Fort Rosalie. The settlement, however, had long since been abandoned. It lay in ruins, its people massacred years earlier by the Natchez Indians.

The trapper took up residence in the abandoned fort and remained there for the rest of his life. He made several more forays into the Chickasaw wilderness to find Red Bone Cave, but never succeeded.

In his later years, the old trapper often visited with the boatmen who plied the Tennessee River. He told them his strange tale of gold bars stacked like cordwood against the back wall of the elusive cavern.

Many thought the old trapper was crazy, but his tale has endured to the present and has inspired hundreds to search for the gold lying deep within Red Bone Cave.

The Miller's Buried Wealth

C. E. Sharps was a well-known trader, landowner, and businessman who operated in and around Florence, Alabama during the 1890s. Sharps not only had a penchant for making money, he had a passion for hoarding it. As a result of his many successful business enterprises and his miserly ways, C.E. Sharps became one of the wealthiest men in northwestern Alabama.

It was not unexpected, then, when Sharps purchased White's Mill. The old mill, which served most of the farmers and residents in the area of Florence, had flourished for many years, and Sharps intended to make it even more profitable. In addition to charging the patrons of the mill a small fee for grinding their corn, Sharps began to make large purchases of the crop, which he ground into flour and sold to the Florence citizens. Sharps also bought about a hundred acres of forest land nearby which he planned to clear and plant with corn and other crops. Though intent on reaping large profits, Sharps also provided important jobs for community residents with his mill and related farming activities.

An quirk of Sharps's was that he always insisted payment for flour or grinding be made with gold coins. Thus the businessman accumulated a substantial fortune in gold over the years.

Always distrustful of banks, Sharps buried his wealth in several locations around Florence. The gold from the operation of the mill was buried somewhere in the forest nearby. Every two weeks or so, Sharps counted the gold he had taken in from the mill, put it in a feed sack, and carried it to a secret location in the forest where he buried it.

Sharps employed his young nephew, Grady Sharps, as an accountant and bookkeeper at the mill. Many times, Grady watched his uncle carry the gold-filled sack out into the nearby woods. The old man always returned without the sack some thirty minutes later.

Grady knew his uncle was burying his wealth somewhere out in the forest, and he longed to know where. Several times, he considered following his uncle, but timidity overcame his greed.

Grady Sharps was a competent bookkeeper and a clear asset to his uncle's business. A family man, Grady often dreamed of the life of luxury a great fortune would provide, but he lacked his uncle's aggressive business orientation. A thin, sallow fellow who looked a bit rodentlike, Grady always seemed content with his life but secretly dreamed of wielding power and possessing wealth.

Once when Sharps left the mill office with a sack of gold coins, Grady followed him to the limits of the mill property. Because C.E. Sharps was known for his violent temper, Grady was terrified to think what might happen if he were discovered. He quickly returned to his desk inside the mill as his uncle, toting the gold-filled burlap sack, disappeared into the dense woods.

Later, Grady actually followed his uncle into the forest. On that day, the young nephew watched as Sharps filled the feed sack with the precious gold coins, tied a knot in it, and left the mill. Replacing his pen in the ink well and closing the account books, Grady waited for a few minutes, then rose from his seat and went to the front door of the mill office. In the distance, he could see his uncle disappearing into the forest. Grady hurried to the place where he had last seen the old man and silently followed his tracks. He stayed close enough to keep his uncle in sight but far enough away so he would not hear him.

Once in the woods and out of sight of the mill, Sharps paused every few steps and looked around to make certain he was not being followed. When he believed it safe, he went on a little way, only to stop and repeat the process again and again.

Each time his uncle paused, Grady was sure he would be discovered. With each step his fear grew, but he knew he was close to discovering his uncle's cache of gold. Finally, though, Grady grew so terrified his uncle would see him that he turned and fled back to the mill. The nephew never found where the uncle buried his wealth, and he never tried to follow the old man again.

By June of 1899, the mill had been in operation under Sharps's ownership and management for several years and had prospered nicely. Sharps decided it was time to make some repairs to the old structure, and he hired several men to do the work.

Sharps was supervising the reshingling of the mill roof one morning, shouting instructions to several of the laborers. While directing a worker, he lost his footing, slid down the steeply angled roof, and plunged into the mill pond some seventy feet below.

Sharps could not swim, and drowned before anyone could reach him. With him went the knowledge of the location of the huge cache of gold in the nearby forest.

For several months thereafter, Grady Sharps retraced his uncle's trail into the forest. Dozens of times he arrived at the spot where he had turned and fled in fear of discovery, but from that point, he could never decide which direction to take. Finally, the nephew gave up in frustration.

The historic White's Mill still stands, a relatively quiet tourist attraction in a picturesque part of Appalachian Alabama. Somewhere, a short distance from the old mill, lies a fortune in buried gold coins, undisturbed for nearly a century.

Lost Silver Mine of the Cherokee

About twenty-five miles east of Birmingham, Alabama, lies a portion of the ancient homeland of the Cherokee Indians. The Cherokee were a relatively peaceful tribe that tolerated the settlement of whites in the area with dignity, forbearance, and friendliness. They often traded with the newcomers.

The Cherokee were distinct from many of the region's other tribes because of the finely crafted silver necklaces and armbands with which they adorned themselves. The ornaments were fashioned from the purest silver ore, and the craftsmanship was the finest ever seen. The origin of the Cherokee silver was often a topic of discussion among whites, but the Indians refused to reveal the secret.

When coal was discovered in the area in 1832 and large-scale mining began, the influx of whites to the region caused concern among the Cherokee, but the Indians stayed friendly and continued to welcome the newcomers.

The new coal mining community was called Ironton. Because of the opportunities available in this booming settlement, it grew rapidly.

Arriving shortly after Ironton's boom was one Dr. Isaac Stone. Though it is doubtful Stone ever attended a medical college, he opened an office, called himself a physician, and proceeded to treat the ills and infections of the community. Stone was quickly successful and was generally regarded as an important citizen of the town.

In 1834, an epidemic of measles broke out among the Cherokee, and the entire village near Ironton was infected. Dozens died and hundreds more were sick and immobilized from the disease. Stone, hearing of the Cherokee's plight, volunteered to travel to the village and treat the Indians. For several days, he stayed with the tribe, ministering to the stricken, until the dread disease finally ran its course, and the tribe was restored to its collective health.

In gratitude, the Cherokee invited Stone to remain in the village for a few days as they prepared a feast and celebration in his honor. The physician agreed and moved into one of the huts.

While tending the sick, Stone could not help but notice the many fine armbands, necklaces, and other jewelry made from silver. He was intrigued by the great wealth to which the Cherokee seemed to have access.

During his stay in the Indian camp, Stone met an elderly Indian named Chief George. Stone and the old man enjoyed each other's company and often engaged in animated talk.

One afternoon, Chief George told him that he held an important position within the tribe—he procured silver from a secret mine northwest of the village. Twice a year, said the Indian, he would select three or four young braves to help him lead a pack train into the mountains to the mine, dig the precious silver, load it onto the horses, and carry it back to the village. There the tribe artisans would fashion the ore into the fine ornaments worn by both men and women.

During a conversation with the old man, Stone tried to learn the location of the mine, but Chief George quickly changed the topic and would not answer the physician's questions. He did, however, make Stone the gift of a silver bracelet.

Several times, Stone purchased cheap whiskey in Ironton and offered it to the Indians in an attempt to loosen their tongues about the silver. His efforts failed.

Finally, the feast and celebration ended, and Stone went back to Ironton. He carried with him, though, an impelling desire to find the rich silver lode of the Cherokee and mine it for himself.

Several months later, Stone told some friends of the secret Cherokee mine. At first they were skeptical of the tale of a rich silver mine, but they were soon won over when Stone showed them the fine bracelet he'd been given.

Stone told his friends that the time was approaching when the old Indian would lead one of the trips to the secret mine to get ore. He suggested hiding nearby and trailing the pack train to the source of the wealth. After the Indians had gotten what they needed and left, Stone told his friends, the men could enter the mine and take what silver they could carry. Stone's friends agreed to join him in locating the mine.

On pretense of checking on the Indians' health, Stone went to the Cherokee village and learned when Chief George would leave for the mine.

Several days later, as the morning sun broke over an adjacent ridge, the old Indian, accompanied by three young braves, led several pack horses from the village as Stone and his companions lay watching, concealed in the nearby woods. When the Indians had a long enough lead, the poachers mounted and followed, staying far enough behind to avoid being seen.

They followed for about three hours and finally arrived at Wolf Creek. There they lost the trail. The tracks of the ponies entered the creek but didn't reappear on the other side, and the gravelly bottom of the fast-flowing stream yielded no clues to the direction the Indians had taken.

Frustrated, Stone and his men separated into two groups and searched both sides of the creek for several miles in each direction. They could find no place where the Indian's ponies had left it.

After several hours of searching, one of the men noticed a curious-looking rock on the creek bank, a rock that seemed out of place. Thinking it had been kicked up by one of the Indian ponies, he dismounted, picked it up, and examined it. Deducing nothing from the four-pound chunk of rock, he casually placed it in his saddlebag and went on with the search.

Late that evening, as Stone and his party convened in the woods at the point where they had first begun tracking the Indians, they saw Chief George and his braves leading the heavily laden pack horses into the Cherokee village! Discouraged, the men returned to Ironton, and Stone never again tried to find the silver.

Several months passed, and the story of the Cherokee silver mine was told throughout the area. Soon, prospectors and treasure hunters were combing the hills near the Indian village in search of the ore. It was never found.

Some time later, the tracker who had found the curious rock retrieved it from his saddlebag. On a hunch, he had it assayed and was surprised to learn it was a freshly mined piece of high-grade silver ore. The discovery spurred a renewed search for the mine, but once again, nothing was found.

When the Cherokee were removed from the region and relocated to Arkansas and Oklahoma, it was said they gathered up much of their fine silver jewelry and ornaments and buried them inside the mine. They sealed the mine entrance and covered it so it would look like the surrounding forest. The leaders of the tribe vowed they would return one day and retrieve the jewelry, but they never did.

Ironton is a ghost town now, and save for the scars of coal mining in the area, there is little evidence that it was once a thriving community. Few people can remember the exact location of the old Cherokee village, but somewhere about a half day's ride from the site may lie one of the richest silver mines east of the Mississippi River.

Flint River Cherokee Gold

Near the southern end of the Appalachian Mountains, in northeastern Alabama not far from present-day Huntsville, a group of Cherokee once settled and farmed a fertile valley adjacent to the Flint River. For centuries, the Indians lived in peace and harmony, raising crops and hunting the abundant game in the nearby forest. The Cherokee, like most Indians, had little use for money and material wealth, so precious metals like gold and silver were useless to them as units of exchange. The Indians did, though, fashion handsome jewelry and ornaments from the valuable metals when they were available.

Legend says that the Flint River Cherokee occasionally traded for gold with other tribes far to the east. The specific source of the gold is unknown, but it is a fact that gold was often found and mined in parts of the Appalachians. Travelers and traders who chanced upon the Indian settlement near the Flint River often remarked on the abundance of gold ornaments and jewelry the Cherokee wore.

As the relentless tide of Anglo settlement flowed into the southern Appalachians during the 1830s, many newcomers coveted the fertile bottomland of the Flint River Cherokee settlement. The earlier friendliness of trappers and traders in the region was soon replaced by the greed and hostility of settlers. When the whites tried to force the Cherokee from their rich farmland, violence erupted, and the Indians repelled the aggressors.

The Cherokee were helpless, though, against the clandestine political maneuvering that eventually forced them off their homeland at bayonet point. Higher powers decreed that the Flint River lands should be opened to white settlement, and the Indians were forcibly removed by the U. S. Army to reservation lands in what was eventually to become Oklahoma.

The journey from the Flint River settlement to the unfamiliar environment of "Indian Territory" was traumatic for the Cherokee. They were soon followed by hundreds of people from other southern tribes also evicted from the ancient homelands and forced to follow what came to be called the Trail of Tears.

Powerless to resist the hundreds of armed soldiers commanded to escort them to the Territory, the Flint River Cherokee made preparations for the long journey.

Because few of the Indians had horses, they would travel on foot, and whatever belongings they took would have to be carried on their backs. Much had to be left behind. Because gold was heavy and of no immediate use to them, the Flint River Cherokee collected all their fine ornaments and jewelry and placed them in a large clay pot. The tribe elders then transported the heavy pot to the edge of the cultivated bottomland and into the nearby woods. In a large clearing, they chose an appropriate place to bury this fortune in gold jewelry.

After the large pot of gold was cached, one of the Indians made cryptic slash marks on several nearby white oak trees.

When they returned to the village, another of the elders made a map on a tanned deer skin. The map showed the location of the village, several important landmarks, and the buried pot of gold. When the map was completed, the maker rolled it up and placed it in a leather bag. The elders agreed that when the tribe was settled into the new lands in the west, they would return for the gold.

The journey along the Trail of Tears was one of terrible deprivation and hardship. Many of the Flint River Indians died of exposure, sickness, and starvation, and it was a decimated tribe that finally reached the assigned lands in the Territory.

Life for the Cherokee was hard in their new home. The men toiled in the fields trying to coax crops from grudging soil, and the women did the best they could to provide decent homes for their families. In time, the Indians, burdened with the fight for survival, gradually lost their enthusiasm for retrieving the pot of buried gold near the old Flint River settlement.

The treasure map prepared by the tribal elder was passed from relative to relative until it finally came into the hands of a Cherokee known only as John. John's grandmother had cared for the map for many years and passed it on to his mother. When she died in 1912, it fell into John's possession.

John grew up in Indian Territory hearing the tale of the buried pot of gold jewelry somewhere near the old Flint River settlement. When he got the map to the treasure, he decided that as soon as he could, he would go to the ancient homeland of his people and try to find the fortune. John had notions of using the wealth to build a reservation hospital for his tribe.

In 1914, when John was fifty, he boarded a train in Indian Territory and made the long journey to northeastern Alabama. He carried only a small pack containing a change of clothes and the treasure map.

Arriving at the little settlement of Ryland, John asked for directions to the old Flint River settlement. He learned the place was now a large farm called Bellfaun and was owned by a man named Shelby Collum. John hoisted his pack over his shoulder and undertook the twenty-mile hike to Bellfaun.

It was early evening when John arrived at the Collum farm and was directed to the main house by one of the farm hands. The Cherokee introduced himself to Collum and told him his reason for coming. He politely asked permission to search the farm for the buried pot of gold jewelry.

Collum, who did not like the looks of the Indian, refused him and told him he didn't want him on the farm.

At this point, John pulled the ancient treasure map from his pack and showed it to Collum. The apparent authenticity of the map softened Collum's attitude, and he asked John to tell him more about the treasure.

John explained the history of the Cherokee gold and told Collum he would share a portion of it with him if he would only relent and let him conduct a search on the farm.

Collum was a shrewd man and not one to pass up such an opportunity. He knew it would cost him nothing to allow the Indian to search the farm, and if the buried wealth were found, it might mean that Collum would share in a magnificent fortune. He agreed to John's proposition. He told John he could spend the night in the barn, and they would begin the search early the next day.

The next morning after breakfast, John and Collum embarked on a search for the gold. John walked in the lead, and from time to time halted and consulted the map for a specific landmark.

At one point, John stopped at a tree and pointed to a very old slash mark low on the trunk. The tree was an ancient white oak, and the cut was partially overgrown—but it was clearly a man-made mark. John pointed to the map, which showed a similar mark.

They found several more trees with similar markings as they walked around the farm. In one particularly thick part of the woods near the edge of Collum's tilled acreage, John found a large tree with the image of a human foot carved into it. John turned in the direction the foot indicated, and after several more paces found himself in a wide clearing ringed by huge white oak trees.

John walked over to one of the trees and found several carved symbols on the trunk, beginning at knee level and extending up as high as John could reach.

The Cherokee regarded the markings in silence for several minutes. Finally, without a word, he turned and walked away, never to be seen again.

Because the Indian left with no explanation, Collum assumed the carvings on the tree indicated someone had returned earlier and recovered the treasure. The farmer gave the matter no further thought until three years later.

While searching for a stray calf in the spring of 1917, Collum came to the clearing he and John had visited three years earlier. The clearing looked much the same—except for an excavation near the center. On closer investigation, Collum discovered a large round hole approximately four feet deep. Weeds growing in the excavated dirt suggested to the farmer the hole had been dug at least a year earlier.

What had been removed from the hole? Farmer Collum pondered that question all his life. Did the Cherokee John return under cover of night and dig up the treasure so he would not have to share it with Collum? Was a treasure found at all? Does it, in fact, still lie somewhere in the clearing in the woods adjacent to Bellfaun Farm?

The mystery has never been solved.

Yuchi Gold of Paint Rock Valley

It was the last year of the seventeenth century, and the small company of Spanish soldiers was about to undertake a most perilous journey, a journey to transport millions of dollars' worth of gold bars across the frontier to a distant point on the east coast of Florida.

For six long years, the Spaniards had labored in a rich gold mine deep in the heart of the Sierra Madres of northern Mexico. The original company of some two hundred officers, soldiers, miners, and priests had been assigned by the Spanish government to extract the precious metal from the grudging rock of the Sierra Madre. The original force had been depleted to sixty by Indian attacks, disease, and starvation, but with the help of Indian slaves, they stayed and continued the mining operation.

At the end of each month, the raw gold was melted down and poured into molds to make brick-sized ingots which were stacked along one wall of the mine awaiting transport to Spain. Sometimes as many as several hundred gold bars would accumulate before an escort from the government leaders arrived.

About three times a year, a big pack train—about sixty mules—would come from Mexico City with supplies. Slaves would then load the bars onto the mules, and the wealth would be taken to the Mexican gulf coast, transferred to a ship, and sailed to the Iberian peninsula.

The officers in charge of the mine began to cast greedy eyes on the gold. After the first year of operation, they agreed among themselves to cache every fifth ingot in a secret hiding place, intending to ship the gold clandestinely to Europe and set themselves up in business. When enough gold had been stockpiled to satisfy the officers, they planned to pack it north, cross the Rio Grande, and make their way to a designated point somewhere on the northeast coast of Florida. Arrangements had been made with a renegade ship captain to haul the riches back to Europe, where the officers intended to live out their lives in splendor.

Sometime during the winter of 1699, the officers decided they had put aside enough gold to make them wealthy men. They were ready to undertake the journey to Florida. The gold was loaded onto pack mules, and the unsuspecting enlisted men were commanded to escort the vast wealth across the continent. Before abandoning the area, the Spaniards executed all the Indian slaves, stacked their bodies in the mine, and sealed and disguised the entrance.

Several days later, the party crossed the Rio Grande near what is now Del Rio, Texas, and proceeded eastward. There were many rivers to cross in the Texas country, and the spring rains had swollen most of them to flood stage, making travel difficult and often delaying the march for days at a time. The Spaniards also had to deal with hostile Indians along the way, and by the time they reached Louisiana, their numbers had decreased significantly. With fewer men, the pack train of some twenty mule-loads of gold ingots was becoming increasingly difficult to maintain.

As the Spaniards neared the Louisiana gulf coast, they learned the Indians in the area were preying on travelers and trappers. Visitors to the region were often tortured, killed, and mutilated. The heads of victims were put on pikes and set in the middle of the trail as a warning to outsiders.

Because of the Indian depredations, the Spaniards made a wide swing northeast and passed through what is now central Mississippi and Alabama. Here they were attacked several times by still other tribes, forcing them to veer even further northeast. Eventually they reached a point just north of present-day Tuscaloosa where the officers ordered a halt so that men and livestock might rest up from the arduous journey.

One evening while the Spaniards were dining around the campfire, a war party of some seventy Indians poured out of the forest and attacked and killed every one of them in minutes.

The Indians were of the Yuchi tribe, closely related to the Cherokee. Ordinarily, they were not warlike, but like most of the other tribes in the region, they resented the encroachment of outsiders on their land.

The Indians, who used gold to make jewelry, led the ingot-laden pack mules back to their village in Paint Rock Valley, about twenty miles east of present-day Huntsville. There, the Yuchi chief ordered the gold stashed in a nearby cave. He did not want any evidence of the intruders' wealth around should his village be visited by friends of the Spaniards.

Over the next several generations, Indians occasionally visited the cave to remove some of the gold for making jewelry, but other than the loss of those small amounts from time to time, the cache remained virtually undisturbed.

During the Indian removal of the early 1830s, the Yuchi tribe was ordered to vacate Paint Rock Valley. Before leaving, many of the Indians went to the cavern and divided some of the gold within. Several families tried to carry some of the heavy ingots on their journey along the Trail of Tears, but they were forced to bury them along the way. Some members of the tribe escaped the military escort and fled eastward to Tennessee with their share of the gold, settling eventually at Henderson Ridge.

The greatest portion of the Spanish ingots remained in the cave.

Sometime in the mid–1920s, an aged Indian appeared at Paint Rock Valley leading two fine mules. He claimed he came from Henderson Ridge and was descended from the Yuchi Indians who had originally settled the valley. The old Indian was impressed with the bountiful farming area that was once the site of the village of his forefathers, and he was friendly to all he met.

The Indian said he was looking for two able-bodied young men to help him load some heavy objects onto the mules, and soon acquired the services of two strapping youths, each about sixteen years old.

The old Indian, the boys, and the two mules left early the next morning and began a long trek out of the valley and into the limestone hills. From time to time, the Indian would call a brief halt while he checked notations on a very old map he carried. About an hour into the journey, the Indian told the youths they would have to be blindfolded the rest of the way. At first they demurred, but the old man said it was the Indian way of doing things, so they humored him and let their eyes be covered. With each of the boys holding onto the tail of a mule, the Indian led the way deeper into the hills.

The men had walked and climbed for another hour when the youths suddenly noticed the air had turned cooler and they could hear the echo of their own footsteps. The Indian removed their blindfolds, and they found themselves inside a great cavern with water dripping from ceiling and walls. The Indian lit a torch, handed each of the youths two burlap sacks, and led them deeper into the cave.

After another twenty minutes of negotiating several big boulders and narrow passageways, they came to a large chamber. Against one wall of the chamber were piled dozens of good-sized rocks, which the Indian asked the boys to remove. They did so and found an irregular jumble of hundreds of brick-sized bars of some kind of metal. One of the boys picked up a bar, hefted it, and suggested it might be lead because of the weight. The Indian merely nodded and asked them to fill the burlap sacks with as many of the bars as they could carry.

The three men made a total of four trips back into the chamber, carrying out burlap sacks containing three or four of the heavy ingots each time. With difficulty, the Indian loaded the bars into several stout leather packs which were tied to wooden pack frames on the two mules. When all the packs were full, the Indian had the boys cover the rest of the ingots with the large rocks they had removed earlier. Though they had carried out several dozen, hundreds still remained in the chamber deep within the cave.

When they were ready to leave, the Indian again blindfolded his two helpers. Assured they could not see anything, he led them back to the valley. The next day, the old Indian was seen leaving the valley leading the two heavily laden mules toward Tennessee. It was the last time he was seen.

Several years later, the two boys—now grown men with families—heard the tale of the rich store of Spanish gold ingots cached in a limestone cavern somewhere back in the mountains surrounding Paint Rock Valley. It was then they realized they had carried gold, not lead, out of the cave for the old Indian.

For many years afterward, the two men tried to find the cave again, but they never did.

The Secret Treasure Tunnel of the Georgia Cherokee

In 1835, the Indian Removal Treaty was signed by the leading Cherokee chiefs, and the long wait for the order to leave their homelands and make the journey to the far west had begun. Before the great migration to what would eventually become Oklahoma, the leaders of the north-eastern Georgia Cherokee plotted to conceal their vast wealth from the greedy white settlers who were moving into the region.

The northern Georgia Cherokee were wealthy even by the white man's standards. For many generations, these Indians had traded with tribes as far away as Virginia. Gold from the rich mines of the Virginia Appalachians was particularly prized by the Georgia Cherokee, and with it they crafted the ornate jewelry they wore.

Shortly before the removal treaty was to be signed, Rising Fawn, the district chief of the northeastern Georgia Cherokee, called a meeting of all the area subchiefs at his home in Settendown Creek. Rising Fawn proposed to construct a tunnel in the nearby mountains and hide all of the Cherokee wealth in it. When the time was right, a delegation of Indians would be sent from the newly assigned lands in the Territory to retrieve it.

All of the subchiefs present at the meeting agreed except for the leader of the Red Bank tribe. For reasons of their own, the Red Bank Indians decided to cache their wealth independently of the other Indians.

Attending this meeting was one Jacob Scudder, a white man who had married into the tribe and eventually became a blood brother and subchief. Scudder, who was not required to leave the area, was appointed caretaker of the Cherokee wealth in the absence of the Indians, an honor which Scudder accepted willingly and with great humility.

Construction of the tunnel began immediately, and each of the subchiefs sent teams of laborers who worked day and night burrowing into the hard rock of the southern Appalachians.

The excavation of the tunnel was to remain a secret from any and all white men (except for Scudder), and when trappers and soldiers visited the area, the digging halted immediately and did not resume until the newcomers had left.

The tunnel was sited in an area completely unsuitable for living, grazing, or growing crops. The ground was rocky, the soil thin, the water scarce, and the timber puny and scattered. In short, it was an area unappealing to the white settlers.

The tunnel itself, when completed, was just over two hundred feet long, and extended deep into a steep rocky outcrop. Along the sides of the long tunnel, the diggers excavated square, room-sized chambers to be used as vaults. Each tribal division was assigned a vault in which to store treasure and other important belongings. The entrance to each vault was a low doorway about three to four feet high.

Soon the announcement came that the Indians were to be removed from their homelands. When word reached the northeastern Cherokee, they had only forty-eight hours to prepare for the long journey. During that time, families carried their gold and other valuable possessions to the secret tunnel. Many walked, with their gold and jewels in packs strapped to their backs; a few came on horseback, leading ponies laden with the accumulated wealth of several generations. Others canoed up the Etowah River to the secret tunnel. Family by family, they deposited their wealth in the tunnel, all intending to return someday to retrieve it.

While the tunnel was being dug, the Cherokee carved and scratched many cryptic symbols on the exposed rocks and outcrops around the region, symbols that allegedly pointed to the location of the hidden treasure.

Coinciding with the removal announcement was a proclamation that in January of 1838, a new federal mint would be opened at Dahlonega, about twenty miles to the north. A gold deposition center had been ordered by the federal government to accommodate the miners, settlers, and soldiers in the area. The new mint required gold bullion for the minting of coins. Most transactions in the region had until then been conducted with gold nuggets and gold dust. All other forms of money were virtually useless there.

According to information gleaned from old Cherokee documents, the Indians robbed an important shipment of gold bound for the new mint. An unescorted wagon carrying the gold was traveling toward Dahlonega from the United States Treasury Department along the old Federal road. Where the road wound through a particularly dense section of forest, five masked Indians halted the coach and relieved it of seven fifty-pound gold bars. It is believed that the robbery was planned by Chief Rising Fawn and executed by five of his most trusted braves. The seven bars were presumably taken to the tunnel and added to an already large fortune.

Not far from Settendown Creek lived two white families. They had settled in the region several years earlier and were friends with the Cherokee. On the evening before the Indians were to leave, while the two families were visiting at one of the homes, the men walked down to Rising Fawn's village to bid the Indians a safe journey and help them load their belongings. The Indians were surprised by the sudden visit of the two white men as they were loading gold for transport to the secret tunnel.

In the center of the village, a large horse-drawn sled with wooden runners stood, piled with jewelry, gold nuggets, bags of gold dust, and other precious artifacts. Several large clay pots were being filled with gold nuggets. Wide-eyed at the sight of such fantastic wealth, the men could only stand and watch.

Rising Fawn spotted the two and led them to a part of the village where they could not see the loading of the treasure. As they talked, the men spotted the sled being pulled away by a team of four horses and disappearing into the forest on the other side of the village. Presently, Rising Fawn and the two men bid each other goodbye, and the farmers left.

Later that evening, the two men decided that after the Indians left the area the following morning, they would go back to the abandoned village and follow the skid marks of the sled, seeking the treasure's hiding place.

The next morning, the two men tracked the sled. For half a mile, the trail was easily followed, but then the tracks entered a shallow creek and vanished. For the rest of the day, the two farmers searched up and down the creek for some sign of the tracks. They never found any.

Just before dawn that day, the last of the Cherokee treasure had been deposited in the vault. Inside the tunnel were several deadfalls. Should anyone but a Cherokee familiar with the tunnel somehow have gained entrance, they would likely have been killed within minutes by one of the traps.

When the wealth was secured and the deadfalls arranged, the opening was filled with large rocks and covered with dirt to make it look like the surrounding landscape.

Jacob Scudder and his family watched with sadness as the last of his Cherokee friends and relatives abandoned their homeland and departed on the infamous Trail of Tears. For many years, Scudder lived in and farmed the fertile valley, all that time watching over the secret treasure tunnel.

Scudder never saw any of his Indian friends return to recover the buried treasure. Occasionally he heard from one of the chiefs, but their messages dwelt mostly on the hard life in the Territory and the continuous fight for survival.

Scudder grew old and finally died at his farm on Settendown Creek. When he passed away, he apparently took with him the secret of the Cherokee treasure tunnel in the nearby mountains.

Searchers since have found many of the carved symbols on the rock outcrops throughout the area, but thus far the cache of gold in the secret tunnel has eluded them.

The Lost Treasure of the Red Bank Cherokee

While most of the northern tribes of the Georgia Cherokee, under the leadership of Chief Rising Fawn, agreed to relocate peaceably to Indian Territory in the west, the Red Bank tribe resisted every effort of the United States government to remove it from its ancient homelands along Bannister and Bruton Creeks in what is now Forsyth County.

The Red Bank Cherokee numbered about one hundred twenty. Fiercely independent, they seldom went along with the dictates of the district chief. Like most Indians in the region, they possessed stores of gold accumulated over the years in trade with tribes far to the east. The Cherokee prized gold solely for its natural beauty and used it only to make jewelry, but when settlers moving into the area showed a preference for the yellow metal, the Indians began to see the ore as an item of barter. After many generations of trade with the gold-rich eastern tribes, a number of Cherokee families had built huge fortunes of gold nuggets and dust.

The Red Bank Cherokee were among the richest of the northern Georgia tribes. When Chief Rising Fawn proposed that all Cherokee conceal their wealth in a secret tunnel and return for it later, the Red Bank tribe alone refused to go along with the plan. *(See the preceding story, "The Secret Treasure Tunnel of the Georgia Cherokee.")*

Always independent, the Red Bank Indians distrusted Rising Fawn and thought him easily intimidated by U. S. Government officials. Likewise, they distrusted Scudder, the white subchief whom Rising Fawn appointed as guardian of the hidden gold. Several of the Red Bank Cherokee accused Scudder of plotting with the whites for the removal of the Indians so that he could secure their abandoned land as well as their abandoned wealth.

As the time for removal approached, the Red Bank Cherokee finally realized resisting the soldiers would be futile, and they relented. The night before they left, the tribe met and decided to bury their gold along the banks of Bannister and Bruton Creeks, mark the spots, and return later for the treasure.

All through the night, the Indians placed their gold in clay pots, chose locations, dug holes, and buried their fortunes. They then carved and scratched locational markers on granite outcrops and stones in the area. One particular stone, an oblong granite boulder weighing more than two hundred pounds, was inscribed with the key to the locations of all the gold caches, believed to number between eight and twenty-five. The total value of the buried gold of the Red Bank Indians is estimated at $2.6 million at today's exchange rates.

Forced to vacate their lands at bayonet point the next day, the Indians put up some mild resistance. After two members of the tribe were executed by the army soldiers, they finally turned and began the long trek to Indian Territory.

Almost a hundred years later, in November of 1932, three boys were playing along the bank of Bannister Creek where it ran through the farm of one F. R. Groover. One of the boys noticed a large, whale-shaped granite rock carved with many curious figures and symbols. The boys had heard the tale of the buried Cherokee treasure many times and decided the rock must mark such a cache.

Suddenly seized by an uncommon sense of propriety for boys that young, the three of them approached farmer Groover and asked permission to dig for gold on his farm. Groover, an intolerant and cranky sort, refused permission and ordered the trio off his land.

That night, the three boys returned to the Groover farm with shovels and picks. With considerable difficulty, they rolled the huge rock aside and began digging. About two feet below the surface, one of their shovels struck a clay pot. Excited, the boys removed the dirt from around the pot, and with an effort, they lifted it to the grassy surface.

The youthful treasure hunters could scarcely contain themselves when they held a lantern above the pot and peered into it. Inside the vessel they found golden jewelry, gold nuggets, and pouches of gold dust. The value of their find was later estimated at $15,540 in 1932 dollars.

Word of the discovery eventually reached Groover, and he soon found the fresh excavation on his farm. He promptly filed suit against the three boys for the return of the gold, which he claimed rightfully belonged to him. Unfortunately for the young treasure hunters, the court found in favor of Groover.

Sometime during the early 1960s, the large stone that marked the disputed cache was obtained by researchers at the University of Georgia and taken to that campus, where it still is. According to the archaeologists who have examined the stone, the carvings of double circles, stick men, and other odd figures describe locations of buried treasure. Unfortunately, finding the locations of the caches of gold depends on the original position of the large stone, and that exact site remains a mystery.

Interviews with many elderly Red Bank Cherokee in the early part of the twentieth century substantiated that the treasure caches could be found by deciphering the markings on the large stone and using its location as a starting point.

Several old-timers who lived near the Groover farm claimed to know the exact location of the stone before it was removed by University of Georgia officials. However, when directions interpreted from the stone were followed, nothing was ever found.

In 1951, before the stone was removed, several Cherokee men traveled from Oklahoma to the Bannister Creek area in search of the stone. They found it, took several photographs of the markings, and spent a week searching for the gold caches. Like previous searchers, they were unsuccessful.

Sam Cranford, an aged part–Cherokee whose grandfather once owned the land on which the Groover farm lay, explained why the searches failed. Cranford told investigators that the point from which the rock was removed was not the original location. He claimed the stone was inadvertently pushed several dozen feet from its original place by a road grader as a road was being widened.

Anyone who knew the original location of the great stone has long since passed away. While the mysterious markings of the stone have been translated, the information is useless as long as its original position remains unknown.

Until then, millions of dollars of Red Bank Cherokee treasure will probably remain hidden not far below ground near Bannister Creek.

The Wandering Confederate Treasury

The spring of 1865 saw the end of the Confederate States of America: it had suffered terrible defeats, its leaders were leaving, and its treasury was rapidly running out of money. Jefferson Davis and his cabinet held their last official meetings in April at Abbeville, South Carolina, and Washington, Georgia, as the group fled encroaching Union forces.

The Confederate treasury, a still-significant store of gold and silver coinage, likewise was moved from the depository at Richmond, Virginia to some undetermined southern location. Some researchers believe the treasure was ordered removed by the departing leaders to protect it. Others of a more cynical nature suggest the deposed leaders wanted the wealth somewhere they might quickly get their hands on it should the nation crumble at the hands of the conquering Yankees.

When General Robert E. Lee told President Jefferson Davis that Grant's forces had penetrated the Confederate lines at Petersburg and Richmond was about to be taken, Davis ordered an evacuation of the region. He assigned William H. Parker to move the treasure.

Parker was a captain in the Confederate navy and took his new assignment quite seriously. On the afternoon of April 2, 1865, with the help of some sixty midshipmen from a training vessel anchored on the James River, Parker loaded the entire wealth of the Confederate treasury into a boxcar. It was to be the first of many transfers. Around midnight, the train departed Richmond bearing an estimated one million dollars. (Some estimates have ranged as high as thirty million dollars, but little evidence has been offered to support those claims.)

When the train reached Danville, Parker received additional orders to move the treasure on to Charlotte, North Carolina, and store it in the abandoned United States mint there. No sooner was this done than Parker learned Stoneman's cavalry was headed in his direction and might be interested in the treasure.

Parker had the treasure removed from the mint, packed in barrels and sacks of coffee, flour, and sugar, and reloaded onto the train. Then, to Parker's dismay, he discovered that the railroads were out of service beyond Charlotte. He hastily transferred the containers onto wagons.

While loading the treasure, Parker learned that Varina Davis, the wife of the Confederate president, was living in Charlotte with her children. Parker found her and persuaded her to travel south with him under military escort before the Union soldiers arrived.

On April 16, the Parker detachment arrived at Newberry, South Carolina. The trains were running, so Parker had the treasure-filled barrels and sacks loaded into another boxcar and continued to Abbeville.

When the detachment reached Abbeville, Mrs. Davis decided to leave the train and stay with some friends who lived in the quiet South Carolina town. Parker was less at ease than Mrs. Davis. Convinced the Union cavalry was hot on his heels in pursuit of the treasure, he wished to abandon the area immediately. He decided to travel on to Washington, Georgia, a few miles across the Savannah River to the southwest. As the train didn't go that way, Parker once again ordered the gold and silver loaded onto wagons. He bid farewell to Mrs. Davis and crossed the river into Georgia.

That part of Georgia had not suffered much from the northern raids, and Parker felt certain he could find a sizeable Confederate military unit that could take over the gold and silver he was transporting in the wagons. The captain was anxious to be rid of the responsibility of the entire wealth of the Confederate nation.

On arriving at Washington, Parker heard that a command of some two hundred Confederate soldiers was holding Augusta, about fifty miles to the southeast. After trading flour and coffee to Washington residents for eggs, milk, and chickens, Parker had his men load the treasure once more in a railroad car, and he ordered the train to Augusta.

At Augusta, the frustrated Parker discovered it was not as easy to reassign the treasure as he had hoped. The officers there informed him the war was over and that they were merely awaiting the arrival of the Union troops to arrange for an orderly surrender of the town, get their pay, and go home. Possession of the Confederate treasury would seriously complicate matters, they informed Parker, and they wanted nothing to do with it. One of the leaders advised Parker to return the treasure to the civilian leaders of the Confederate government, who at that very moment were fleeing Union soldiers across the Savannah River into Georgia. Among those in flight was President Jefferson Davis himself.

Mistakenly, Parker decided Abbeville would be the likeliest place to find Davis to ask him what to do with the treasure. He believed Davis knew his wife was there and would try to find her. The fastest route to Abbeville was back through Washington, so the captain ordered the train to return. There, the monotonous task of loading the gold and silver onto wagons was once again undertaken, and the journey to Abbeville was underway.

Less than an hour out of Washington, Parker, much to his surprise and chagrin, encountered Mrs. Davis and her children fleeing Abbeville with a small cavalry escort. She told Parker that she had not seen her husband and had no idea where he was.

On April 28, Parker and his command finally arrived at Abbeville, unloaded the wealth from the wagons, stored it in an empty warehouse just outside town, and placed a heavy guard around it.

That evening as he was dining, Parker received word from one of his scouts that a large contingent of Union forces was a few miles north of the town and would arrive soon. Panicked, Parker ordered his men to reload the treasure into a railroad car. He ordered the engineer to prepare to depart, but before the train could be started, several hundred soldiers appeared at the north end of the town, riding straight for the train.

Fortunately for the harried Parker, the soldiers turned out to be a Confederate company escorting President Davis and what was left of his cabinet. Parker greeted Davis and related his misadventures with the Confederate treasury. To his great relief, Davis ordered the responsibility for the gold and silver transferred to the acting secretary of the treasury, John H. Reagan. Almost as quickly, Reagan transferred the responsibility to John C. Breckinridge, the secretary of war. Breckinridge, not excited about the burden of responsibility for the wealth of the Confederate nation, passed it to General Basil Duke. Duke had no one to pass it on to, so he assumed the assignment with his customary rigid military bearing and dignity.

Duke was one of the few remaining Confederate generals, and his command was a motley assortment of nearly a thousand poorly armed and equipped volunteers who were deserting in droves. When the soldiers learned the war was over, several at a time would simply slip away and return to their farms throughout the devastated south.

Around midnight of May 2, Duke urgently ordered the wealth transferred once again from the boxcar to several wagons. Duke had learned earlier in the evening that Union patrols were thick in the area, and he would be lucky to transport the gold and silver farther south and away from the advancing Yankees. Duke believed Union officials were aware the treasure was in the area and were determined to seize it. With a force of about a thousand Confederate troops, Duke moved the treasure out of Abbeville in the dark of night. Jefferson Davis and his remaining cabinet, grateful for the escort, rode along. Several of the troops stayed far to the rear of the column keeping an eye out for pursuit, and dozens more rode along the flanks prepared to ward off an attack by the Yankees.

During the rest stop around midmorning of the next day, May 3, Duke promised his soldiers that when they reached Washington they would be paid in gold from the treasury they were escorting. Knowing the war was over and anxious to be on their way, the troops clamored for payment on the spot. The soldiers were also concerned that Union troops might suddenly appear and seize the money before they could get what they were due. For the rest of the day, Duke and a paymaster counted out thirty-two dollars to each soldier in the command.

This done, the wagons were escorted across the Savannah River toward Washington, Georgia. Every few minutes, Duke got word that Yankee soldiers were only minutes away from attacking his column. At the first opportunity, he ordered his command to leave the trail and take refuge in a large farmhouse belonging to a man named Moss. The barrels and sacks of gold and silver were unloaded from the wagons and stacked in the farmhouse kitchen. Duke then stationed his men at strategic points around the farmhouse, ready to hold off a Yankee attack on the traveling treasury. The attack never materialized.

The Confederates spent the night at the farm, very few of them sleeping since they anticipated trouble at any moment. When scouts reported the next morning that no Yankees were in sight, Duke ordered the treasure reloaded onto the wagons, and it was carried into Washington without incident. At Washington, Duke turned the wealth over to Captain Micajah Clark, whom Jefferson had earlier that day, in his last official act as president of the Confederacy, appointed treasurer of the Confederate States of America. Then Davis, along with his wife and children, fled deeper into the south. They were captured six days later.

Captain Micajah Clark decided that his first obligation as Treasurer was to count the money. According to the Treasury record, the exact amount was $288,022.90. It was considerably less than what Parker had left Richmond carrying, and through the succeeding years, there has been much speculation as to what happened to the rest of the money.

Parker, writing some thirty years later, suggested that Clark may have submitted a false accounting of what was turned over to him and kept the difference.

Many believe that Jefferson Davis, before turning the treasury over to Clark, appropriated much of the wealth and fled with it, burying portions of it in several locations before he was captured.

In any event, Clark paid off a few more soldiers out of the funds and had the rest repacked in kegs and wooden boxes.

On May 14, two officials representing a Virginia bank arrived in Washington with a federal order for the total amount of the treasury. The bank apparently held a claim on the wealth, and the two men were commissioned to secure it and return it to Richmond.

Following the military order to the letter, Clark turned the entire treasury over to the two bank representatives who in turn had it loaded onto wagons and, under protection of a military escort of some forty soldiers, left for Richmond.

Most of the soldiers in the escort were young, and very few had seen any action during the war. For that reason, the two bank representatives were nervous throughout the trip. Soon after the column left Washington, a scout reported they were being followed by a gang of outlaws made up of discharged Confederate soldiers and local hooligans. The soldiers were ordered to take extra precautions as the small wagon train lumbered toward the Savannah River.

Travel was slow, and on the afternoon of May 24, the party pulled into the front yard of the home of the Reverend Dionysius Chenault, only twelve miles out of Washington. The wagons were pulled into a large horse corral and drawn into a tight defensive circle. The guard was doubled and posted about the corral that night while the rest of the command tried to sleep.

Around midnight the outlaws struck. Firing only a few shots, they surprised the inexperienced federal guards, who quickly surrendered. The guards were tied up, and the remaining soldiers, who awakened at the first sound of gunfire, were held at gunpoint by several of the outlaws. The leaders of the gang smashed open the kegs and boxes containing the gold and silver coins and stuffed their saddlebags full of the booty. Thousands of dollars' worth of Confederate wealth was spilled onto the ground as the greedy outlaws filled their pockets. Finally, carrying all they could hold, they mounted and rode away on horses barely able to carry both treasure and rider.

One of Reverend Chenault's daughters estimated that well over a hundred thousand dollars' worth of gold and silver coins was recovered from the ground the next day.

The outlaws rode northwest to the bank of the Savannah River. Learning they were being pursued by both Confederate soldiers and local law enforcement officials, they hastily dug a pit and buried their wealth in a common cache, intending to return for it when the pursuit was abandoned. A company of soldiers reportedly encountered the bandits the next day and killed all of them. The incredible wealth of gold and silver coins is believed still to lie buried on the south bank of the Savannah River.

Members of the Chenault family hurriedly gathered up the fortune in coins that had spilled onto the ground during the robbery. Placing the gold and silver into kitchen pots and wooden crates, they buried it adjacent to a nearby tributary to the Savannah River. No representatives of either the Confederate or Union government ever returned to the Chenault farm to claim that treasure.

The Reverend Chenault cautioned his family against digging up the treasure until such time as the passions of the war died down and it would be safe, but it is believed the treasure was never recovered.

Searchers for the treasure buried on the Chenault farm are routinely disappointed to learn that the small tributary near where it was cached has been inundated by the waters of Clarks Hill Lake. According to the U.S. Army Corps of Engineers, the Chenault portion of the Confederate treasure lies beneath some thirty feet of water.

Cohutta Mountain Gold

There is gold in the Georgia Appalachians, and lots of it. Eons ago, when the great mountain range was taking shape, tectonic forces deep beneath the crust were activated. Molten rock under tremendous pressure fought to break through the crust and spread out over the landscape, but the crust held, keeping the magma trapped beneath thousands of feet of rock, where it began to cool. The suppressed volcanic material eventually hardened to form granite and related rock. Scattered here and there within the vast underground bodies of igneous intrusive stone, impressive veins of gold-filled quartz formed.

As centuries turned into millennia, and millennia into several-million-year geological epochs, pressures within the earth forced some of the granite masses closer to the surface. Ages of erosion by wind and water removed hundreds of feet of sedimentary deposits, eventually exposing the ancient granite.

As streams flowed across the exposed granite, eroding the coarse surface particle by particle, entrapped minerals were exposed. Early Indians who settled in this region often found gold in these mountains, sometimes in great quantities. They mined it, stored vast amounts of it, and used it primarily for ornaments and jewelry.

When white trappers and traders arrived in the Georgia Appalachians, they saw the fine gold of the jewelry with which the Indians adorned themselves, and they craved its ore.

Soon prospectors and miners came, rediscovered some of the gold, and established mining enterprises. When most of the Indians were removed from the region in the 1830s, greedy and enterprising whites moved into the lands formerly held by the Indians and began extracting the riches from the rock.

Several tales of vast gold deposits have come from the area around Cohutta Mountain, about two-and-a-half miles east of Chatsworth, Georgia, near the Tennessee border.

Prior to the Indian Removal of the 1930s, a man named William Hassler built a grist mill on the creek that still bears his name. Hassler had settled in the region several years earlier and made friends with the Indians living nearby.

The largest of the Indian villages was spread out over the flood plain of Hassler Creek just east of the mill. Hassler ground corn for the Indians and also traded items he shipped in from Virginia. When he first began dealing with the Indians, he saw that they had a lot of gold, and he asked them to pay with that metal.

Whenever the Indians ran low on gold, Hassler noticed, three or four of the elders would leave the village and travel along the creek upstream toward Cohutta Mountain. They were usually gone for three or four days, and when they returned, they carried leather ore sacks filled with gold nuggets that looked to be cut from a rich vein.

Hassler suspected that the Indians had a rich gold mine back in the mountains, and he was determined to discover its location. One day when he saw four tribal elders departing for Cohutta Mountain, he called for one of his slaves. The miller told the slave, a mere boy, to follow the Indians at a discreet distance and try to find their gold mine.

All day long the young slave followed the trail, staying well behind the elders and just out of sight. When he reached the base of Cohutta Mountain, he lost sight of the Indians and could not locate the trail. As he searched the ground for some sign of passage, the four Indians appeared out of the surrounding forest and encircled the tracker. They told him if he ever followed them again, they would kill him and all of his family. The Indians then marched the young slave back to the mill and presented him to Hassler with the same warning. With that, the elders departed, trotting back toward the mountain. Several days later, they were seen returning with more sacks full of gold nuggets. The Indians carried on trade with the miller as if nothing had happened.

With the death threat hanging over him, Hassler never again tried to find the secret gold mine on Cohutta Mountain.

Many years later, during a lull in the War Between the States, two soldiers named Pence and Wells were granted a short leave to return to their homes near Cohutta Mountain to round up hogs. As best the story can be reconstructed, the men were hiking along a small stream on the mountain when they discovered the old Indian gold mine. Each man dug several ounces out of a large gold-laced vein deep inside the mine and then, pockets full, continued their search for the stray hogs.

Once all the hogs were found, the two men had to return to their military unit. They put the gold in a shot pouch and hid it in the hollow of a chestnut tree on the mountain. They planned also to return to the mine for more gold after they had served their time in the Confederate army.

In the ensuing months, Wells was killed in action and Pence was wounded badly enough to merit a discharge. The trauma of the war apparently affected Pence's mind to the degree that he had difficulty sleeping and remembering things. His neighbors claimed he had simply gone crazy from his experiences in the war.

After several months, Pence had marginally recovered from his wound, and decided to make the long hike to the chestnut tree of Cohutta Mountain and retrieve the pouch of gold. He planned to cash in the ore, buy mining equipment, and extract more gold ore from the old Indian mine.

Pence searched for several days but couldn't find the chestnut tree. He claimed that the tree was no longer there, but it is likely that he simply couldn't find it again.

For the rest of his life, Pence tried to find the ancient Indian gold mine. Years of fruitless searching made him completely lose his mind, and he was eventually sent to an institution. To the last, Pence never wavered from his tale of the rich gold mine he and his friend Wells had discovered that day.

Around the turn of the century, an old Cherokee Indian showed up in the town of Chatsworth. The old man was little more than a derelict, clothed in tattered rags and obviously hungry. He tried to get work at several places but was chased away. On his second day in town, he struck up a conversation with a group of men and told them that if they would give him six hundred dollars, he would lead them to the ancient Indian gold mine on Cohutta Mountain.

Two men, James Mullins and Jim Sellers, knew the story of the mine, and they agreed to take the risk.

The next morning, the Indian led Mullins and Sellers to Cohutta Mountain on horseback. For a day and a half, they traveled up ravine and narrow valley, into regions the two men had never seen. As they rode, Mullins and Sellers carefully noted landmarks so they could return to the mine, should it be found, without the help of the Indian.

Midway through the second day, the three men rode right up to the gold mine. In two hours, Mullins and Sellers dug enough gold from the exposed vein to fill their saddlebags. The old Indian tended the horses and watched as the men carried their new-found wealth from the mine.

When their packs were filled, they followed the Indian out of the mountains and back to Chatsworth. Pleased with their investment, Mullins and Sellers paid off the old

Indian, who immediately left town and was never seen again.

Mullins and Sellers got rich from selling the gold they had brought back from the old Indian mine, but nine months later, their money was gone. They organized a second trip to Cohutta Mountain and the gold mine.

On the morning of the second day out from Chatsworth, Mullins and Sellers got lost. They recognized none of the landmarks on trails, were hopelessly confused, and eventually returned to Chatsworth without finding the mine. The two men tried several more times, but always failed.

During the 1930s, a man named Fletcher prospected on and around Cohutta Mountain. Fletcher was originally from England and had come to the United States to seek his fortune in the gold fields of Georgia. By the time he arrived, however, most of the mining operations had closed down. Undaunted, the Englishman decided to try his own luck at prospecting and mining and settled in the Cohutta Mountain region, believing that the exposed granite hills still held the promise of gold.

After many trips into the mountain, Fletcher returned from one with a sackful of gold he claimed to have dug out of an old abandoned mine. The gold was very pure, and the sale of it made Fletcher rich.

Later, Fletcher fell ill and was given only days to live. Just before he died, he asked that his bed be taken outside where he could gaze upon the mountain. He gave the remainder of his fortune and a description of the mine to a friend who had ministered to him during his illness. Fletcher told him that inside the mine was a thick vein of quartz woven with one-eighth-inch thick strands of pure gold. Fletcher gave directions to the mine, but the friend could not remember them.

A few days later, Fletcher passed away, and the secret of the last gold mine of Cohutta Mountain apparently died with him.

The Lost Slave Gold Vein

Jacob Scudder, longtime friend and ally of the Cherokee Indians, was a prosperous Cherokee County farmer. He owned hundreds of acres of rich Georgia bottomland, raising on it bountiful crops of corn and fine herds of cattle and horses.

Slaves worked Scudder's farm. The farmer was reputedly kind and fair to his workers, fed them well, and saw to it that they were never overworked in the fields. When gold was discovered in the county during the 1840s, Scudder even allowed his slaves to pan for gold after their day's work was done. The only restriction he placed on them was that they had to give him the first option to purchase their gold. In this way, Scudder gained a great deal of gold, and many of his slaves bought their freedom.

One of Scudder's most valued workers was a slave named Black Dan Riley. Black Dan was in his forties, soft-spoken, and a competent and valued field hand. The other slaves looked to Black Dan as their leader, and he was often their spokesman when important issues arose.

Scudder and Black Dan got along very well, and when the slave approached the farmer about purchasing freedom for himself and his wife, Lucinda, Scudder readily agreed. Scudder offered to set Black Dan up as a sharecropper, providing him with a piece of land on which he could build a cabin and raise livestock of his own. Black Dan and Lucinda agreed to stay.

Gold fever was running through America then. Gold had been discovered in Virginia several years earlier, prompting a rush of people into the area and creating several boom towns in the rugged Appalachians to the northeast. Just two years earlier, gold had been discovered about two miles southwest of the Scudder farm, and miners and opportunists from as far away as New York and Pennsylvania were flocking to the northern Georgia Appalachians to pan independently or work for the newly created Franklin Gold Mining Company or establish businesses.

In 1849, gold was discovered in California. The promise of instant wealth was so great that easterners flocked to the Golden State in droves. Many of the men working for Georgia's Franklin Mines pulled up stakes and joined the great westward migration.

While Black Dan Riley had had some success in panning for gold in the small streams of Cherokee County, he longed to try his luck in the California gold fields. The fever burned hotter as he watched several of his friends pack up and undertake the long journey to California.

While farming his sharecropper plot and dreaming of California gold, Black Dan kept panning in the small streams near the Scudder farm. One day, he crossed one of Scudder's wide cornfields to reach a narrow creek that marked the eastern boundary of the property. Black Dan had not worked the little stream before and was anxious to see if it had any potential.

As he panned likely spots, Black Dan could see slaves working Scudder's cornfield on the other side of the stream. Once in a while, one would wave at him, and he would wave back. Black Dan kept panning, gradually moving upstream.

At a gentle bend in the stream about fifty yards up, Black Dan found some color in his pan. Fifteen minutes of working the site rewarded him with some tiny nuggets. Feeling lucky, he moved a little farther up the stream and began panning another site. He found several more nuggets, and this time they were larger, coarser, and more numerous.

He moved upstream and excitedly panned another spot. Again he found even larger, coarser nuggets—so large and plentiful, in fact, that he could actually see them lying in the bottom of the stream bed.

Black Dan knew enough about gold to know he was getting close to the source, most likely an exposed vein higher up. For most of the day, he panned his way carefully up the stream, feeling sure he was closing in on the source of the gold.

Finally, he reached a spot where his efforts yielded no gold. Deducing that the vein was somewhere between where he then stood and the last place he had panned, some thirty yards downstream, he began his search.

Black Dan walked up and down both sides of the stream several times and found nothing, so he decided to pan the stream every ten feet or so until he isolated the source. Eventually, he narrowed his search to a length of about twenty feet.

On one side of the stream, the land sloped upward, and patches of exposed rock could be seen along the bank. Black Dan focused his attention on these outcrops. Digging near the bottom of one, he found the top of a thick vein of quartz. Carefully brushing the dirt away, he discovered pure gold densely laced throughout. Here, at last, was the source of the gold in the stream.

As Black Dan dug several chunks of the ore from the rich vein, he pondered his future. The desire to go to California still burned in his heart, but he also believed he had stumbled onto a small fortune in gold right at his fingertips. He decided to go home and speak to Lucinda about the matter, and together they would decide.

Before leaving the site, Black Dan carefully covered over the exposed quartz vein and pocketed the day's yield. He walked home.

That evening over supper, Black Dan and Lucinda agreed to travel to California to try their luck in a new place. If they were not happy there, they would return to their northern Georgia farm and dig the gold there.

The next day, Black Dan sold his gold to Scudder for seventy dollars, bid the farmer farewell, and took off for California, Lucinda with him. Scudder wished his friend luck and invited him to come back if the California adventure proved unsuccessful.

But Black Dan did well in the California gold fields. He filed on several claims, all of which richly returned gold ore. After three years of panning in the California mountains, Black Dan and Lucinda had an impressive sum of money. Tired of living in primitive conditions in the mountains, they moved to a big city on the California coast where they lived comfortably for the next twenty years.

When they were in their sixties, Black Dan and Lucinda began to miss their old home in Georgia. They spoke often of the simple life and the slower pace they remembered in the Appalachian hills. By this time, they had spent most of what had been earned in the gold fields, but they still had enough money left to be considered wealthy by anyone's standards.

They returned to Georgia and settled onto a piece of land not far from where Black Dan once sharecropped for Scudder. Scudder had passed away years earlier, and others had taken over his farm.

One day, Black Dan gathered up his gold pan and a shovel and set out for the small stream and the gold-filled quartz vein he had discovered more than twenty years earlier. He found the stream with no trouble, got his bearings, and walked to where he remembered the vein to be. As he climbed the slight incline to the upper reaches of the stream, he noted that during the twenty years he was away, the landscape had changed considerably. Much of the woodland he remembered had been cut down and turned into pastures. The little stream had shifted its course in several places and looked much different. And where before there had always been a strong flow of water, the creek now only held a trickle.

Black Dan panned parts of the little stream as he searched for the quartz vein. He was rewarded with some fine dust in the bottom of his pan, but nothing like he had found twenty years earlier. He tried to remember where he was standing when he waved at the slaves working in Scudder's field so long ago, but everything seemed so different now. Black Dan was confused.

When Black Dan reached the place where he thought the rich quartz vein was, he dug into the sloping hillside under one of the rock outcrops. He found nothing. He dug in several more places, but still no quartz. Discouraged and tired, the old gentleman went home, planning to try again the next morning.

The next day was no more fruitful. Panning in the stream sometimes yielded small amounts of gold, but Black Dan was not satisfied. He longed to find the rich vein.

Months passed. At least twice a week, Black Dan could be seen exploring the little stream in search of the elusive vein. When he grew too old to dig, he hired a boy named Carnes to accompany him. He told young Carnes the story of his lost gold and promised to share it with the lad if they found it.

Black Dan showed Carnes how to pan the gold out of the stream and taught the boy much of what he knew about the gold mining business. For months they searched the low hills around the little stream, but the quartz vein eluded them.

Black Dan Riley died without ever finding his vein. For several years, Carnes continued to search for the gold he firmly believed must exist near the stream at the base of one of the outcrops, but he never found it.

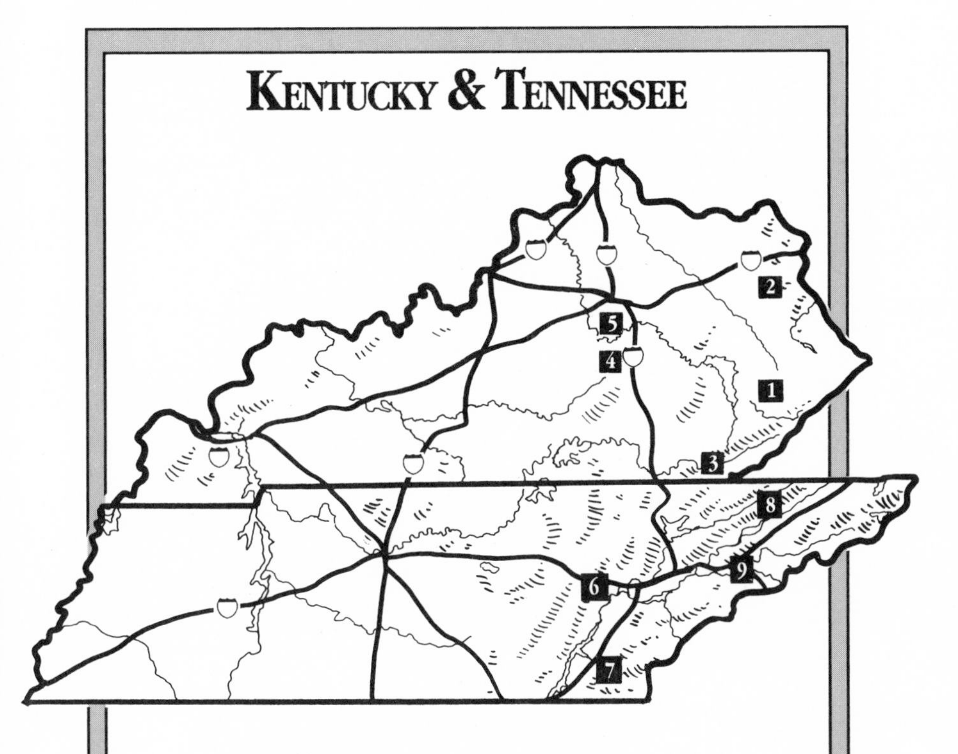

KENTUCKY

1. The Lost Jonathan Swift Silver Mines
2. Lekain's Fabulous Treasure Cache
3. The Lost Silver Mines of the Melungeons
4. Buried Bank Robbery Loot at King's Mill Dam
5. General John H. Morgan's Buried Treasure

TENNESSEE

6. Secret Silver Mine of the Cumberlands
7. Tasso's Field of Confederate Gold
8. Buried Union Army Payroll
9. The Cave of Gold Above Elk River

The Lost Jonathan Swift Silver Mines

Throughout the Kentucky Appalachians, abundant evidence can be found of ancient mining and smelting of silver ore. Some of the long-abandoned mines were dug by Spanish soldiers under Hernando de Soto. The French also mined silver from these Appalachian rocks during their occupation of the new world.

When the Spanish and French departed the region, Shawnee Indians, many of whom had previously been enslaved by the whites to work in the mines, continued extracting the precious ore. Occasionally, Cherokee Indians who wanted the silver would raid the Shawnee and take temporary control of one or more mines. For almost three hundred years, millions of dollars' worth of silver was extracted from these rich mines.

Into this setting arrived one Jonathan Swift in 1760. Little is known of Swift's background. It is believed that he came from England to the United States around 1750. He claimed a sailor's background but bore himself like an educated gentleman. Speculation arose that Swift had been wanted for piracy and other crimes on the high seas and that he had sought refuge in the colonies to evade capture and possible execution. It is known that Swift served for a time with General Braddock during the French and Indian War in 1755.

After mustering out of the British army, Swift wandered to the bustling cities of Washington and Alexandria on the Potomac River. It was in Washington that Swift met George Mundy and learned of the rich silver mines of the eastern Kentucky Appalachians that would forever be linked to his name.

For one so young, George Mundy (whose name is given in some accounts as "Alfred Mundy") had already experienced a lifetime of hardship and a heartstopping array of adventures. Mundy had been a mere boy in 1752 when he accompanied a party of trappers into the eastern Kentucky wilderness. The men were trapping and trading for hides and pelts which they planned to sell in the larger cities in the east. While camped in what is now Wolfe County, one of the trappers shot and wounded a bear, which sought refuge in a nearby hole in the rock wall of a mountainside. The trapper ordered young Mundy to enter the cave and tie a rope around the bear's legs so it could be dragged out. As Mundy, grass torch in hand, crawled on hands and knees through the narrow opening, he discovered it was actually the entrance to a long-abandoned mine. Curious, he moved deeper into the shaft. At one point, the light from his torch reflected off a thick vein of glistening silver along one wall. Noticing his torch was nearly burned out, Mundy returned to the entrance and told the others what he had found.

The trappers, excited about getting rich off their discovery, immediately began enlarging the tunnel and mining the ore. Their skills were primitive and their efforts clumsy, but they soon dug out a large quantity of silver. As work progressed in the mine, the men occasionally noted Indians watching them from the nearby ridgetops. Since the Indians never approached or threatened, the trappers saw no need to post a guard.

One morning, as several woodsmen were loading sacks of silver ore onto their horses in preparation for departure, they were suddenly attacked by the Indians. After a brief and futile defense, all the woodsmen were killed except for young Mundy. During the fighting, the boy hid in the mine, where he was discovered by the raiders. Because of his youth, Mundy was taken captive to be raised by an Indian family and used as a slave.

Mundy soon learned his captors were Shawnee, and that they operated silver mines of their own there, both where Mundy had found the mineshaft and in the nearby Red River gorge. He, along with other slaves, was taken to the Red River valley region and made to work in the Shawnee silver mines for several hours each day.

One day, the Shawnee camp was raided by a large force of Cherokee. The invaders scattered the Shawnee, fired the village, and made captives of Mundy and several Shawnee youths. Mundy soon learned that the Cherokee had silver mines of their own, for they quickly put him to work in them. The Cherokee occasionally dug ore from Shawnee mines in secret, he also discovered.

Once, a party of Spaniards visited the Cherokee while they were camped in a wide valley. Leading three large ox-drawn carts, the newcomers brought mining tools and maps of the region. The Spaniards remained in the village with the Indians for several weeks, and with the aid of the Cherokee, found several of the old silver mines that had been abandoned and covered over during the de Soto expedition. From these mines, the Spaniards took great quantities of ore, gradually filling the ox carts with the treasure. From the Spaniards, Mundy learned something of the history of the mines in the area.

While exploring this region around 1542, de Soto's scouts heard of rich silver mines in the mountains. Local Indians told the soldiers the mines had been operated for centuries by the tribe. The Spaniards visiting the Cherokee village more than two hundred years later had detailed reports on the locations of these long-abandoned mines and the amount of silver that was taken out and shipped back to Spain as ingots. The Spanish and the Cherokee, with Mundy and a small number of other slaves, worked together to dig more of the ore from the nearby mines.

When the Spanish had gotten all the silver they could carry, they left the village and headed southeast. Several weeks later, a group of French soldiers visited the Cherokee village. Like the Spaniards before them, the French were welcomed. The French also knew of the rich silver mines and had come to ask the Indians if they could mine them. Mundy learned that the amicable relationship between the Cherokee and the French stemmed from an alliance committing the two to driving the British and Americans from the region. The silver from the rich Indian mines was financing the French army.

In 1754, the British general Edward Braddock was sent into the Kentucky wilderness, where he engaged the French and Cherokee in a savage battle. George Mundy, allied with the Indians, fought for the French in several skirmishes, and was eventually captured by Braddock's army. The young man was taken to Alexandria, Virginia. After being questioned about movements and affairs of the Indians, he was released. Mundy, with no means of support, wandered the streets of Alexandria begging for handouts. It was there he met Jonathan Swift.

Swift felt sorry for the young man who had endured so much and then been cast out to fend for himself on the sometimes wicked streets of the city. The former soldier invited the lad to live in his home and treated him as if he were his own son. In return, Mundy willingly served Swift as a valet and developed a fierce loyalty to him.

Some time after Mundy moved in, Swift had to sail for Cuba on business, and he left the young man in charge of his home. When Swift returned to Alexandria several weeks later, he and Mundy became close friends, and at that point, Mundy shared with Swift the story of the Kentucky silver mines.

Swift was enthralled by the tales of the wealth in silver that Mundy claimed could be found in the far-away Kentucky Appalachians, and his heart fairly burst with excitement as he thought of the fortune waiting in the remote wilderness of the far mountains.

Mundy told Swift that after the skirmish with the British soldiers, the Indians had abandoned the mines and the French had been driven from the area. There was enough silver, the young man claimed, to stock the treasuries of several nations. As Swift's mind reeled, Mundy offered to guide him to the mines.

Swift began preparing for a journey to the abandoned silver mines in far-away Kentucky. He sailed once again to Havana to secure the services of two competent miners he knew, named Gries and Jeffrey. Returning to Alexandria, Swift gathered around him several men with whom he had served in Braddock's army: Samuel Blackburn, Isaac Campbell, Abrom Flint, James Ireland, Shadrach Jefferson, and Harmon Staley.

Finally in late spring of 1759, financed by Swift and guided by young Mundy, the party left for the Kentucky Appalachians. On this and subsequent trips, Swift maintained a journal, and it is from his writings that much of the information concerning the silver mines has been gleaned.

With some difficulty, Mundy guided the men to an area in what is believed to be present-day Floyd County. On arriving, the young man seemed confused and cast around for a myrtle tree thicket that he said was near the entrance of one of the richest mines in the region. The following account appears in Swift's journal:

> On the first trip, Mundy got lost. We put our horses on the river called "Red." We put them in a place surrounded by cliffs and fastened to the entrance with grape vines. We crossed the river to the other side and wandered all day and came back from where we started from. The next day Mundy said he could go down the river to the Indian trace. He would know the way then. He went down the river two or three miles west and found the Indian trail. So we wandered all that day and next. Late in

> the evening, Mundy hollered out, "Here is the myrtle thicket. I know the way now."
>
> We went down a flight of Indian stair steps at the top of the cliff and crossed to the other side. We climbed up and went 200 yards on the second ledge and found the opening to the mine.

For many weeks, the party dug the plentiful silver from the mine. They made a crude furnace and smelted the ore, fashioning it into ingots. Soon the miners had more silver than they could carry on the horses and mules. Swift suggested they return to Alexandria, convert their silver to cash, and organize a second and larger expedition.

About a year later, another expedition was formed, including Swift, Mundy, Blackburn, Gries, Ireland, Jeffrey, and Staley, along with newcomers Henry Hazlitt, Joshua McClintock, and several Shawnee Indians.

On the second journey, according to Swift's notes, Munday took the men to a different mine somewhere in what is now Bell County. This mine proved to be even richer than the first, and they spent nearly seven months mining the ore and converting it into ingots. Winter was approaching, and Swift decided it would be wise to leave the wilderness and return to the east. As they had more silver than they could possibly take back, they hid hundreds of ingots in the mine shaft and in nearby caves and rock niches. The group arrived in Alexandria on December 10, 1760.

While resting in his adopted city, Swift contacted one Seth Montgomery, a British merchant who owned and operated a small fleet of trading vessels that plied the Atlantic between England and America. Montgomery formerly worked as an engraver for the Royal Mint of England, where his specialty was cutting dies and coining golden crowns, England's principal exchange medium in the new-world colonies. With his wealth, Swift bought into

Montgomery's trading enterprise, and the two purchased five more ships.

Once this new business was operating efficiently, Swift organized a third expedition into the Kentucky mountains. Montgomery accompanied the party on this trip, and they departed Alexandria on June 25, 1761.

The group journeyed by way of Fort Pitt (now Pittsburgh) where they were joined by more Shawnees and several Frenchmen. Swift had learned of increased Indian depredations in the wilderness and believed a large party of well-armed men would offer greater protection.

The expedition eventually arrived at the forks of the Big Sandy River near present-day Louisa in Lawrence County. Here the party split up. Half of them, led by Mundy, traveled up the west fork to locate new mines. The others, led by Swift, journeyed to the same mine they had worked the previous year.

Each group labored to extract ore and convert it into ingots. Apparently Montgomery, with his knowledge of dies and coinage, supervised the making of illegal British crowns. According to Swift's journals, thousands of the coins were fashioned and stored in barrels brought along for that purpose. Collectors now hold several of these coins.

Swift, Montgomery, and a few others departed for Alexandria, arriving on December 2, 1761. The rest of the party continued the mining and smelting operation. Swift and Montgomery took with them several mule loads of silver ingots and coins, and when they arrived at Alexandria, they immediately purchased an additional two ships for their fleet. Onto these ships were loaded goods bound for England from the colonies, and though it has never been proven, many suspect that barrels of English crowns molded in Kentucky crossed the ocean, too, and were used by the partners in business transactions. Hundreds of the illegal coins are also suspected to have been introduced into the colonies soon after Swift and Montgomery returned.

The two returned to Kentucky around the last week of March, 1762, bringing a large pack train of supplies. Arriving again at the fork of the Big Sandy, Swift traveled southward along the base of Pine Mountain to the Cumberland Ford in what is now Bell County. Here he organized the opening of several new mines and prepared to spend the winter.

The winter of that year, however, was unusually harsh, and the men were forced to quit the region. Several tons of silver bars and coins were loaded onto the pack animals, and the party returned once again to Alexandria, arriving on December 1, 1762. Along the way, according to Swift's journals, thousands of dollars' worth of silver had to be cached to make travel easier.

In Alexandria, Swift and Montgomery purchased more ships, expanding the size of their trading fleet to a small navy. Furs and other trade goods, along with several barrels of illegal English crowns, were loaded onto the ships and carried to England. Shortly after the vessels returned, Swift, Montgomery, and the others went back to Kentucky.

Regular trips to the Kentucky mountains to mine the silver continued until 1769. On the final expedition, the party left for the mines on October 9, and once they got there, split up the ore, ingots, and coinage that had previously been cached and returned to Alexandria on December 11. It was the last time Swift was to visit the mines.

According to Swift's journals, millions of dollars' worth of silver was taken from the mines while he operated them. On several occasions during return trips, some of the wealth had to be cached. Once, under attack by Indians, the travelers had to abandon large amounts of coins and ingots, hiding them in rock niches. On other occasions, pack animals became crippled and whatever portion of the silver they were transporting was hidden in nearby rock caves or buried near some prominent landmark with the intention of later retrieval. Swift's journal entry of September 1, 1767, reads:

> ...[W]e left between 22,000 and 30,000 dollars and crowns on a large creek running near a south course. Close to the spot we marked our names (Swift, Jefferson, Mundy, and others) on a beech tree with compass, square, and trowel.
>
> No great distance from this place we left 15,000 of the same kind, marking three or four trees with marks. Not far from these we left the prize near a forked white oak and about three feet underground, and laid two long stones across it, marking several stones close about it. At the forks of the Sandy, close by the fork, is a small rock house with a spring in one end of it. Between it and a small branch we laid a prize under the ground; it was valued at 6,000 dollars. We likewise left 3,000 buried in the rocks of the rock house.

A later journal entry, recorded in Swift's rather cryptic style, gave directions to the mines in the Red River gorge area:

> If you strike the creek below the furnace keep in the creek searching diligently for a big rock house on the left hand side about 100 yards from the smaller rock house the furnace is in, the creek makes a bend or turn to the south and there is the fallen rock in the creek near the bend. If you discover the furnace go to the middle mine, go up over a southeast course until you come to a remarkable hanging rock very high up with a gap in between it and a very large mountain, within 100 yards you will find a line of rocks the mine is in.
>
> The last trip we came we saw our mine was so immensely rich it was decided by our party to abandon the mine for three years for me to go to England and get a party interested to come over here and work the mine on a large scale.

In 1770, Jonathan Swift left America for England. As stated in his journal, he intended to attract investors and skilled miners and engineers to return to the Kentucky wilderness with him and operate the silver mines on a grand scale. Swift had planned to remain in his home country for a while, but his stay turned out to be much longer than he expected. One evening while quaffing ale in a pub, he was overheard berating the king and his foolish colonial efforts in the new world. Swift was seized and thrown in jail for his vocal American partisanship, and there he languished for nearly fifteen years. While in prison, Swift began to lose his eyesight, and by the time he was released, he could not discern objects more than forty feet away.

When Swift finally returned to America, he discovered that many of his friends, including Mundy, had attempted a return to the mines the previous year and were never heard from again. They were believed either killed by Indians or perished in the unusually bitter winter. Swift had difficulty locating the others, but finally found McClintock. These two men, together with a ragtag party of several Indians and two Frenchmen, left Alexandria in 1790. They intended to travel along the old trails to the mines and recover some of the hidden wealth. Converted to working capital, this could be used to finance a larger expedition to reopen the mines.

Swift, half blind, couldn't find the landmarks he needed to relocate the silver mines. So rapidly was Swift's eyesight failing that a companion had to lead the once hale sailor, outdoorsman, and miner by the arm. Several times, the party found trees and rocks blazed with marks identifying nearby caches of coins or other wealth, but Swift could not see well enough to lead his men to the precise locations.

Though the small party searched many weeks for the mines and the buried caches of silver, they found nothing. When provisions finally ran low, Swift suggested they return to the east. In Alexandria, he lived out the rest of his life, alone and blind, and finally passed away in 1800.

While geologists and hard-rock miners have found silver in varying quantities in the Kentucky Appalachians, the many rich mines of Jonathan Swift remain hidden. Some suggest that when Swift and his men abandoned the mines, they went to great lengths to seal the entrances and camouflage them so they would look like the surrounding environment. Though hundreds have searched the rugged hills and mountains of eastern Kentucky, the Swift mines have eluded all.

Some who have studied the history of the Swift silver mines suggest they never existed and were a product of Swift's imagination, a cover for the alleged coin counterfeiting operation. Swift's silver, the argument continues, was actually plunder from his oceanic trading ventures, which supposedly were nothing more than a cleverly disguised piracy operation. According to the critics, Swift carted stolen silver chalices, plates, and jewelry into the wilderness, melted them down, and minted illegal coins from them.

Researchers have found no documentation linking Swift to piracy. Furthermore, it is not logical that Swift would travel hundreds of miles into the remote and rugged Appalachians to melt down stolen silver when he could more easily have done so only a few miles from Alexandria.

Most likely, the Swift silver mines did indeed exist, and produced an incredible fortune for the men who worked them. The evidence for the existence of these mines is plentiful and has been found in Bell, Estill, Jackson, Lee, Morgan, Powell, and Wolfe counties. Old furnaces have been discovered in these areas, and studies show they were used to smelt silver. Many caches of old mining tools have also been found, tools of mid-eighteenth century vintage. One cache of tools contained a hand-cast hammer bearing the inscription "JC Blackburn." Blackburn was one of Swift's miners. Several rock engravings bearing the names Swift, Mundy, and Jefferson have been found near the furnaces.

Historians for the most part agree the Swift silver mines existed. They are still lost today probably because they are in remote areas, they were likely concealed when abandoned, and the forest and undergrowth have encroached on the sites so they are almost impossible to identify.

The search for the rich silver mines continues, and the same passion for discovery and for great wealth that imbued the adventurous Jonathan Swift more than two centuries ago still beats in the hearts of modern-day treasure hunters.

Lekain's Fabulous Treasure Cache

In the year 1750, a half-breed Frenchman named Howard Lekain traveled up the Mississippi and Ohio Rivers from his Louisiana home in response to tales he had heard about the possibility of mining gold and silver in the Kentucky Appalachians. Lekain followed dozens of other Frenchmen who had gone to the area in search of wealth.

At that time, the French claimed all the territory west of the Allegheny Mountains. Because of this French dominance and because the French were on friendly terms with most of the Indian tribes in the region, Lekain and his countrymen passed easily through the area in their quest for silver and gold. So friendly did Lekain become with the local Indians that he eventually married into the tribe.

On one of his prospecting forays, Lekain discovered a very rich vein of silver near the present-day town of Carter, in Carter County. With the help of a dozen Indian workers, the Frenchman excavated a substantial amount of ore. In addition to the rich silver strike, Lekain found a significant gold deposit nearby. In the years that followed, Lekain built up a fortune as he mined and stored precious metals.

Once his mining operation was under way, Lekain built a furnace to smelt the ore into ingots. Besides the bars of silver and gold, he made some crudely formed coins of a Spanish design which he successfully used as currency in the region.

As years passed and word spread about the wealth that could be found in the Kentucky Appalachians, more and more Frenchman came to try their luck at mining. People from the eastern colonies also sought new lands in this area to farm and colonize. The encroachment of whites into their homeland and hunting grounds angered the local Shawnee Indians. Hostilities grew between the two cultures, and small raids eventually led to full-scale warfare.

Before long, whites could not move about the area without risk to their lives, and Lekain began to fear for his and his wife's safety. He decided to go back to Louisiana until the warring passions cooled.

Unable to transport his entire fortune of gold and silver, Lekain loaded as much as he could onto his wagon and made plans to cache the remainder in a safe place.

With the help of his Indian friends, Lekain packed ingots into six wooden kegs and coins into two one-gallon buckets. Then he examined several of the many caves in the area and chose one suitable for caching his fortune. The cave had a small opening and was located just across Tygart Creek from the settlement. From the cave entrance, one could see Cedar Cliffs rising above the creek. The narrow passageway wound down at a forty-five degree angle through a fifteen-foot layer of hard-packed clay and gravel and into a limestone formation. After about forty feet, the passageway opened into a chamber some thirty feet long and twenty feet wide with a ceiling averaging six feet in height. In the center was a large rock which had evidently fallen from the limestone ceiling.

With the help of his Indian laborers, Lekain hauled the kegs and buckets of ore into the chamber and put them against the far wall. He collected several of the limestone rocks that littered the floor of the cave and stacked them up around his treasure. Then he scraped dirt from the floor of the cave onto the mound of rocks, covering them entirely. To a stranger accidentally entering the subterranean chamber, the cache would look little different from the uneven floor of the cave. When this was done, Lekain, with the point of his knife, carved his name and the year—1774—on the side of the large rock in the center of the chamber. When the Frenchman and the Indians left the cave, they placed a large flat rock over the the opening.

By this time, back at the settlement, the wagon was loaded and ready for departure. Because an attack from the Shawnee was imminent, Lekain's Indian friends implored him to leave the valley as soon as possible. However, the Frenchman lingered near the cave another hour to sketch a map showing the location of the cave, noting prominent landmarks such as Cedar Cliffs, Ring Rock Spring, and Tygart Creek. Lekain also wrote a lengthy description of the treasure, the cave, and the area, all in French.

Before leaving, Lekain etched the outline of a snake on a nearby rock so that the head of the reptile pointed directly at the opening of the treasure cave.

Satisfied, Lekain and his wife climbed aboard the wagon and, accompanied by twelve Indians, headed north out of the Appalachian valley toward the Ohio River, where they hoped to get a boat and return to Louisiana.

On the evening of the second day of travel through the dense forest, the small party was attacked by the Shawnee. While Lekain's Indians fought off the attackers, the Frenchman and his wife fled through the woods into the darkness.

Weeks later, the two arrived in Louisiana. The Frenchman felt it prudent to wait until the Indian hostilities in the Appalachians subsided before going back to his mine, so he settled into subdued family life in his humid homeland.

The following year, a daughter was born to Lekain. While he relished the role of family man, he was anxious to return to the Appalachians and retrieve his treasure. Unrest in the region continued, though, and he feared for his safety. When Lekain's daughter was four, the Frenchman was struck with a fever from which he never recovered. He suffered for days lying abed, watched over by his wife, before passing away one night in his sleep.

Before he died, Lekain gave the map and directions to the treasure cave to his wife and told her to try to retrieve the fortune.

Lekain's wife had become too accustomed to the comfortable life in Louisiana to undertake a long journey to the rugged Appalachians. The map and the description were stowed away and forgotten.

When Lekain's daughter grew up, she married a man named Tinder. They had one child, a son they named Robert, and when Robert was grown, he accidentally discovered his grandfather's treasure map among some family belongings.

Robert Tinder lived in Kansas, and did not have the money to leave and search for the treasure the map said lay in the cave in the Kentucky wilderness. Tinder waited, and over time, saved money toward a journey to retrieve the treasure.

Sometime in 1819, a Kentucky settler accidentally found Lekain's treasure cave—but missed the gold and silver.

John Butler was farming part of the floodplain near the Meadow Fork of Buffalo Creek, an area now called Wesleyville. Butler and his wife built a crude log cabin on this site, gradually adding to it over the years as he tilled the rocky soil and grew corn and raised hogs and cattle. By 1840, Butler's log cabin had evolved into a fine home, a handsome accompaniment to his now-prosperous farm. Over the years, Butler added acres to his once meager holdings and became noted for his fine crops and good horses.

One winter morning, Butler found a dead colt near his barn. The animal had been partially devoured and there were two sets of mountain lion tracks leading away from it. Enlisting his fourteen-year-old son, Butler followed the lion tracks in the snow north for several miles across rocky terrain. Later in the day, as Butler and his son neared Tygart Creek, they discovered the lion tracks ended at the edge of a large flat rock on a hillside. On closer examination, Butler saw that the rock partially covered a cave opening just large enough to allow a supple panther to wriggle inside.

Butler and his son pried the rock away from the hole with a stout oak limb. Butler fashioned a crude torch of dry bark gathered from some hickory and cedar trees, and together the two entered the small cave to dispatch the livestock-killing lions.

On hands and knees, the trackers negotiated the first forty feet of the cavern before reaching a chamber where they could stand. Rifle ready, Butler held the torch high. Near the back wall crouched two young lions, their eyes aglow with the reflection of the flame. Butler shot them both.

After examining the dead lions, Butler and his son explored the small cave. The first thing he noticed was a large rock in the center of the floor that bore the inscription "LEKAIN, 1774." Butler assumed the carving was done by some wandering hunter.

Idly curious, Butler was staring at the mound of dirt heaped near the back of the cave when a shout from his son distracted him. The boy had discovered a shovel near the front of the chamber, and the two began searching the cave for other tools. As the torches burned low, Butler decided it was time to start the long hike home.

On leaving the cave, Butler and his son spent about an hour rolling rocks and boulders into the entrance to discourage any further use by mountain lions. They filled the entrance, then rolled a large boulder across the opening, completely covering it.

Some years later, Butler and his family moved to Kansas, where in a curious twist of fate, they became neighbors of Robert Tinder, the grandson of Lekain. Tinder later married Butler's daughter, and the couple eventually had two children.

As he grew older, Butler began to lose his eyesight and contented himself with sitting before the hearth telling stories of the old days in Kentucky. Tinder was visiting the Butler home one evening when the old farmer recalled tracking the mountain lions to the partially concealed cave near Tygart Creek. He told of killing the lions and finding a rock in the cave with the name "LEKAIN" scratched onto the surface.

Tinder listened intently and soon realized this was the same cave indicated on the old deerskin map in his possession! He retrieved the map, and as Butler described the region around the cave, found corresponding landmarks on it. Tinder then told Butler the story of his grandfather's buried treasure, a fortune in gold and silver that Butler had walked past as he explored the cave.

The desire to travel to Kentucky and find the treasure cave fired Tinder, but he could not afford to leave Kansas then. Years passed, and Tinder, then approaching sixty, was finally able to make the journey from the windswept fields of the prairie to the rocky remoteness of the Appalachian backwoods.

When Tinder reached the valley of the treasure cave, he met a farmer named Wash Stamper, who lived near Olive Hill. He told Stamper why he had come to the area and showed him the map and other documents penned years earlier by Howard Lekain. As Tinder spoke, Stamper recognized the landmarks indicated on the map—Cedar Cliffs, Ring Rock Spring, and Tygart's Creek. Stamper listened closely to Tinder's tale and told him he knew the exact location of the rock on which the snake had been carved, and that furthermore he knew the exact location of the cave of which Tinder spoke. Stamper, like everyone in this valley, was familiar with the story of farmer Butler tracking the mountain lions to their den, killing them, and then filling in the opening.

With little difficulty, Stamper led Tinder to the cave entrance, still sealed with rock and dirt and covered by the boulder. Tinder decided the rock and soil could be removed easily enough and hired several men for the job. By the afternoon of the second day, much of the fill was gone from the cave entrance and passageway.

The work was difficult because it rained throughout. A small stream of water flowed into the opening, turning the loose clay into an unstable slurry. About eight feet of passageway had been cleared and one of the workers was lowered by rope to the farthest extent of the excavation. As the worker tried to remove more of the packed clay and rock, the opening caved in, nearly killing the man. The rest of the laborers considered it folly to continue trying to open the dangerous passageway, and after a brief discussion, they all quit. During the evening, the rain washed more clay and rock into the opening, completely refilling the entrance.

Frustrated but undaunted, Tinder decided to sink a wide shaft straight down into the chamber of the cave from higher on the hillside. They easily excavated an opening about sixteen feet wide in the thick layer of soil, and reached the limestone formation that made up the bulk of the mountain. Several feet of the rock had been blasted and removed, for a total depth of twenty-five feet, when Tinder received word from Kansas that his wife was seriously ill and not expected to live. Work on the shaft halted while he made the long journey back to Kansas to begin a vigil by her bedside.

A year later, Tinder returned to the Tygart Creek area to resume excavating the shaft. His renewed efforts were set back by a lack of workers, funds, and competent engineering.

Robert Tinder died in 1903 still trying to locate his grandfather's cached fortune. He was buried near Tygart Creek. Members of the Stamper family still live in the area. According to them, people still come in search of Lekain's fortune, but there has been no concerted effort to gain entrance to the chamber where gold and silver still lie under a simple mound of rock and dirt.

The Lost Silver Mines of the Melungeons

Early in 1770, a strange and secretive group of travelers moved into and settled a portion of the Cumberland Mountain region of the Appalachians near the point where Kentucky, Tennessee, and Virginia share borders. Within a few months, the newcomers discovered silver and began to mine a very rich vein of the ore. The mining was carried on for several generations.

Most of the silver taken from the mines was made into coins which were used as a medium of exchange throughout the region. When the federal government began to pressure the so-called counterfeiters, the transfer of the coins became more difficult. Eventually the mines were closed, and the mysterious residents of the region turned to farming and distilling spirits. The mines, believed to be somewhere near Pineville, contain not only an incredibly rich vein of silver but also an estimated three million dollars' worth of coins and ingots said to have been cached in one of the passageways in 1794. The location of these productive mines has remained a mystery for nearly two centuries.

The odd settlers, who were the first non-Indians to penetrate the Cumberland Valley, were called Melungeons, and their origins are shrouded in mystery. Local legend, most of which has been gleaned from the Melungeons themselves, suggests a Portuguese ancestry, but this has never been verified.

One story is that sometime around 1768, several families chartered a boat to carry them from the port of Lisbon, Portugal, to America, where they hoped to establish a settlement. During the long, difficult voyage across the Atlantic Ocean, the ship's officers and crew tried to rob and kill the passengers, but the travelers fought back fiercely, subduing the sailors and throwing them overboard. They then comandeered the craft and guided it to the North Carolina shore, where they beached it. Fearing pursuit from allies of the ship's crew, the colonists retreated westward deep into the mountains, eventually reaching and settling the region just south of Pineville, Kentucky.

Few residents of the American colonies were aware of the arrival of this group of people in the country, and even fewer were aware of their settlement in the remote Cumberland River valley. Consequently, the migrants lived contentedly in relative obscurity for many years.

The name "Melungeon" has been described as a corruption of a foreign word, the meaning of which is lost to history. Though they have referred to themselves as "Portogee," at least one historian has suggested the Melungeons might be of mixed French origin.

Physically, the Melungeons appear more Mediterranean than northern European. They were described in a Tennessee Historical Society report of 1912 as having a swarthy complexion, straight black hair, black eyes, and heavy-set body structure.

So completely did the Melungeons dominate the area they settled that they eventually became a law unto themselves. During the early 1800s, a time when migrants from the eastern colonies sought new lands to settle in the Appalachian wilderness, the Melungeons repelled intruders with a fierce determination that often ended in the newcomers' deaths. They soon had a terrifying reputation, and the knowledgeable traveler avoided the region. On those few occasions when fearless and hardy families tried to start farms in nearby valleys, a horde of Melungeons would sweep out of the hills, steal cattle and other livestock, and set fire to barns and houses.

As time passed and more families came to settle in the region, law enforcement followed. The growing population and accompanying officers of the law subdued the warlike Melungeons, and the hostilities diminished. Eventually, the clan became less of a menace to homesteaders and turned to distilling whiskey and brandy and selling it in the area. For many years, the Melungeons were famed for their fine brandy, and it is believed their skill in producing it originated in their European homeland. Occasional raids and plundering forays continued, however, and the Melungeons remained a relatively serious threat as late as the onset of the War Between The States. It was not until around 1885 that area residents considered it safe to cross Melungeon territory.

Not long after settling in the Cumberlands, the Melungeons discovered silver. It is believed they found several abandoned mines that had once been operated by Spaniards, Indians, or both. The Melungeons excavated the silver for several decades. Their silver mines are believed to be located in the area of Straight Creek, a small tributary which joins the Cumberland River near the present-day town of Pineville.

As settlers began moving into the area and towns and communities started springing up, the Melungeons were quick to realize the value of coins as a medium of exchange. Using handmade dies, they fashioned their own currency and introduced it in the region in exchange for staples, cloth, and farming implements.

Locally-minted money was generally accepted in many of the more remote regions of this newly settled country. Silver was hard to come by, and shopkeepers were happy to obtain it in the form of coinage, no matter what the origin. Throughout much of the Appalachians, homemade coins fashioned from the ore of area mines commonly entered the local economy.

As Kentucky, Tennessee, and North Carolina were granted statehood and came under the laws of the United States, transactions involving locally minted currency became illegal, and the federal government sent agents into the mountains to confiscate such coins and see to it that production was halted. (Interestingly, the Melungeon coins actually had a higher silver content than the coins made at the United States mint!)

When the U.S. government shut down the local manufacturing of coins, the Melungeons abandoned their mines. A portion of the estimated three million dollars' worth of silver ingots and nuggets that had accumulated over the years and not been used to make Melungeon coins was divided up among the various families. The bulk of the wealth, according to legend, was stacked inside one of the mines. To inhibit prospectors, fortune-seekers, and the merely curious, the Melungeons sealed up the entrances to the shafts.

That the Melungeons did have access to a great wealth of silver cannot be disputed; local history fully documents it. In addition, James Adair, an Englishman who wrote of his travels through the Cumberland region in 1775, mentioned that the Melungeons (whom he described as "desperate vagrants") were seen carrying horseloads of silver into Georgia to purchase slaves.

Around 1900, a farmer searching for stray cattle in the valley of Straight Creek discovered furnaces which had apparently been used to smelt ore. The trees growing out of them suggested the furnaces had not been used in years, and residents of the area hadn't known they existed. Historians believe the Melungeons built these furnaces to smelt their ore. Nuggets of silver have also been found in the area, and some experts claim they actually came from one of the mines and were dropped during transport to the furnaces.

The fascinating history of the Melungeons has been researched over the past hundred years, but little more is known of them now than when the studies began. A relatively shy people whose society was rather closed, the Melungeons have successfully avoided scrutiny. The few who have been interviewed have revealed little.

The lost silver mines of the Melungeons, now covered with rock and forest debris in a seldom-traveled area near Straight Creek on the Cumberland Plateau, remain as elusive as the culture that mined them.

Buried Bank Robbery Loot at King's Mill Dam

The year before the War Between The States was fairly peaceful in most of central Kentucky, and hints of the impending violence were obscured by the tranquility and serenity of the Appalachians. The population in the western foothills of the range was growing steadily as settlers came from the east to establish small farms. Communities sprang up throughout the region, and as the population grew, new businesses and banks appeared among the buildings in the young settlements.

Nicholasville was one such community, comfortably nestled in the rolling hills near the Dix River some fifteen miles south of Lexington. It was toward this slumbering town that four sinister-looking men silently rode one early spring morning as the sun rose above the eastern mountains.

The riders, three just barely out of their teens and one about forty, gently coaxed their horses across the Dix River just above the King's Mill dam. The mill, powered by the diverted stream, ground area farmers' corn into fine meal for baking. Where the four men crossed the river, they could look downstream and barely see the outline of the mill through the slowly thinning fog.

Following a seldom-used trail, the four stopped just within the protection of the thick woods overlooking Nicholasville. As the sun climbed, merchants began to bustle about the streets readying their businesses for another day.

The attention of all four watchers focused suddenly on the bank as a black-coated, bowler-hatted, middle-aged man walked to the front door of the cut-stone building and bent to insert a key into the massive lock. Several minutes passed after the man entered the bank, and presently the riders saw the window curtains thrown open. After another five minutes, the oldest rider uttered a quiet command to approach the town.

Moving casually, yet with purpose, the four men passed through the community, stopping in front of the bank. The older rider glanced up and down the main street, and when he was satisfied the foot traffic was light and inattentive, he and two of the young men dismounted and handed their reins to the fourth rider, who stayed on his horse. Though proud of being given charge of the mounts, the young outlaw cast jerky, nervous glances all around as his three companions entered the bank.

In less than a minute, gunshots were heard from inside the building, and the three outlaws emerged, two of them laboring to carry a wooden chest. The third bandit mounted, and the others lifted the heavy chest so that the two riders could carry it between them. At once, they turned their horses and fled toward the forest from which they had come minutes earlier. The other two bandits had no sooner mounted and spurred their horses in the wake of their fellows when the banker came running into the street screaming that he had been robbed.

The first two riders had difficulty managing the heavy chest they carried between them. Twice they dropped it, and it was slowing their escape so much that the older man, fearing their pursuers, suggested they carry it to the Dix River, bury it somewhere along the bank, and come back for it later.

At the river bank, the four hurriedly dug a shallow hole, deposited the chest, covered it, and fled downstream just as a mounted posse broke through the woods in hot pursuit.

The fleeing bandits rode for the Dix River cliffs and sought shelter among the rocks. As the posse approached, the bandits opened fire. Dozens of shots were exchanged for several minutes, and then a silence fell over the area. Thinking the bandits killed, the posse members cautiously entered the rocks only to find the robbers had fled. The pursuers found no tracks leading from the hiding place and gave up the chase.

Back at Nicholasville, the banker told authorities that the stolen chest had contained several thousand dollars' worth of gold coins in one- and five-dollar denominations. He described the chest as being of fine cedar, bound with metal straps and corners.

Several years later, a man lay near death on a bed in a rooming house in Lexington. A consumptive, the man could scarcely breathe, and it was clear he would not live another night. The proprietress of the rooming house, along with a few of the boarders, tended to the sick man's needs as best they could, but their efforts were futile. Late that afternoon, the dying man beckoned the woman, and when she approached, he weakly pulled her toward him and whispered a confession. With the last of his energy, the man admitted his part in the Nicholasville bank robbery. He gave such clear and precise details as to leave no doubt that he had been there. He told the woman that, while fleeing from the posse, he had paused to bury the chest along the Dix River bank not far from the King's Mill dam. He told her the chest contained a fortune in gold coins, and he wanted her to have it as a reward for her kindness to him.

The confession was reported in area newspapers, and soon treasure hunters were digging every square foot of the Dix River bank near the old mill. Nothing was found, and the chest of gold remained lost until 1910, when it was finally discovered.

George Kelley, a local blacksmith and fishing guide, was diving for fish in the King's Mill Pond when he saw the treasure chest under about fifteen feet of water.

Kelley recognized the old chest for what it was immediately, but he was surprised to find it at the bottom of the pond. The chest was made of one-inch-thick cedar boards held together with metal straps and corners, and had clearly been designed to transport coins or bullion. The box had rotted so badly that some of the wood fell apart when Kelley tried to move it. After several dives and with considerable difficulty, Kelley finally got the chest to the nearest shore. Pulling the lid open, the blacksmith discovered some gold coins in the bottom of the chest. The others had apparently fallen through the many holes in the wood.

Because of the location and description of the chest and the pre–Civil War dates on the gold pieces, historians believe the strongbox was the one taken in the Nicholasville bank robbery about fifty years earlier.

When George Kelly found the chest and the coins, the decades-old story of the Nicholasville bank robbery was recalled by area newspapers, starting a steady stream of treasure hunters to the King's Mill pond over the next several weeks. Nothing more was discovered, for Kelley refused to say exactly where he had found the chest.

What of the other coins that supposedly had filled the old chest? George Kelley had a theory. The blacksmith believed the part of the tale about the outlaws burying the chest along the bank of the Dix River. He also believed that a sudden rainstorm and runoff eroded the river banks and uncovered the chest. Kelley thought that once the chest was uncovered, the force of the surging stream waters pushed it farther into the river, and gravity eventually pulled the old box to the bottom of the large pond. Over the years, the water and mud decayed the cedar boards.

As the wooden chest rotted and the wood decayed, Kelley theorized, the coins spilled out onto the bottom of the pond. Given the weight of gold and the softness of the muck, he believed the coins sank deep into the thick, silty bottom of the pond. The coins Kelley found in the chest when he pulled it to shore were all that remained of a vast fortune.

Under fifteen feet of water and who-knows-how-much muck at King's Mill Pond, an incredible fortune in gold coins may rest just beyond the reach of searchers.

General John H. Morgan's Buried Treasure

For many years, John H. Morgan was the pride of the Confederate Army. His record of command, leadership, and bravery was noteworthy, and it was inevitable he would some day be promoted to general. General Morgan conducted several successful raids for the Southern army, seizing needed horses, arms, and funds to support the Southern effort in the Civil War. They added to Morgan's stature as a military genius and encouraged influential politicians to regard him as a future contender for high political office.

Morgan always succeeded beyond expectation, earning lavish praise from his peers. While lower-ranking officers were placed in charge of confiscated horses, guns, and ammunition, General Morgan himself controlled a rapidly growing fortune in gold, silver, and currency.

As the end of the war approached, Morgan's career declined as a result of some poor military decisions. The tremendous wealth he gathered during the numerous raids was never entirely accounted for and is believed to be hidden along roads and trails the Confederate forces once traveled. It is estimated that Morgan accumulated nearly one million dollars in gold and silver bullion and both Union and Confederate currency during the time he commanded a Rebel battalion.

As this impressive fortune grew, Morgan had it packed and lashed onto several stout horses which, under heavy guard, stayed with his command. With each raid, with each sack of a town, with each addition of monies from county treasuries and town banks, the packs grew larger and the pack horses more numerous.

Morgan also extorted large sums of money from local businessmen and farmers who lived in and near the towns he raided. Accompanied by a well-armed contingent of cavalry, Morgan would ride up to a business or home and threaten to burn the structure unless a ransom was paid.

It is not certain when Morgan intended to deliver this rapidly growing fortune to the treasury of the Confederate army, for as he gathered more and more wealth, he became less and less inclined to part with it. He took great pride in his laden pack horses and bragged often to his contemporaries about transporting this treasure along with his army during his military campaigns.

As the Union army steadily advanced during 1863 and the Confederate forces weakened, Morgan suggested to General Bragg that several large cavalry raids in the north might divert pressure from the Rebel troops. At the same time, said Morgan, more money could be secured along the way to fund the Confederate cause.

At first Bragg was hesitant, but because the Confederates were both losing battles and running out of money, he finally relented and allowed Morgan to lead a command to the north. He cautioned Morgan, however, to keep his forces on the south side of the Ohio River. Morgan agreed, but had no intention of following Bragg's orders. In fact, the general looked forward to raiding and looting the cities of the north.

With a command of 2,460 men, Morgan advanced from Tennessee into Kentucky on July 1, 1863. All along the route, Morgan's army looted and pillaged towns, farms, communities, and travelers. It is said that Morgan even robbed the collection boxes at local churches. While these new funds were intended to aid the Confederate cause,

Morgan and a few of his staff always seemed to spend a great deal of the money on themselves. Morgan and his followers dined well on fine meals and expensive wines, attended by servants.

During the campaign, Morgan's army struck Salem, Kentucky, raiding and looting like bandits. The cavalrymen were so intent on acquiring goods and destroying the town that they paid little attention to the orders of their commanding officers. There was fighting, killing, raping, burning, and drunkeness, and it became clear that Morgan was losing control of his command. After the Salem raid, Morgan had trouble maintaining discipline.

During that raid, hundreds of rifles were confiscated along with thousands of dollars. The guns and ammunition were shipped south to Confederate troops in Tennessee and Virginia, and Morgan added the money to his growing wealth.

On July 12, Morgan led his forces into Versailles, Kentucky. Attacking the small town on that warm, still morning, Morgan personally led a raid on the county treasury and pocketed in excess of five thousand dollars.

Disobeying Bragg's orders, Morgan crossed the Ohio River, and his force swarmed into Ohio, raiding and looting the towns of Jasper and Piketon. As on previous raids, Morgan's undisciplined soldiers vented their fury on these towns, behaving more like a mob than trained cavalrymen.

The continued breakdown of discipline and vigilance brought tragedy on Morgan's army. On July 18, a portion of Morgan's command was intercepted, attacked, and captured by Federal forces, leaving the general only nine hundred soldiers. Massive Union forces were closing in on Morgan from several directions. Morgan, normally a brilliant military tactician, ignored warnings of the impending attack. The only precaution he took was to add extra guards to his pack train.

On July 26, the Ninth Michigan Cavalry launched an attack on Morgan's army at Salineville, Ohio. Thirty Confederate soldiers were killed in the first few minutes of battle, fifty more were wounded, and two hundred were captured outright. Realizing a crushing defeat was inevitable, Morgan, along with several fellow officers and his heavily guarded pack train, fled the battle scene, traveling south toward the Ohio River. Slowed by the cumbersome load, Morgan and his group were captured near West Point, Ohio. None of the treasure was in his possession when he was overtaken, and it is believed the wealth was buried somewhere along the escape route.

Morgan and his fellow officers were held at the state penitentiary at Columbus, but the general had no intention of remaining a prisoner for long. Within days of being jailed, Morgan organized an escape plan. Using tableware for digging tools, he and his men excavated a tunnel and escaped on the evening of November 26, 1863. Traveling at night, Morgan and his followers eluded their pursuers and reached the safety of the Confederate lines far to the south.

After his capture, Morgan's prestige began to wane. Though he was now largely ignored and avoided by Confederate leaders, he did manage to obtain command of a force of twenty-five hundred cavalrymen for a raid on Kentucky.

Departing from a location near Pound Gap, Virginia, Morgan led his raiders at a rapid pace some one hundred fifty miles into Kentucky, arriving at the town of Mount Sterling on the morning of June 8, 1864. Following a brief battle, the small town was easily taken, and Morgan, apparently learning nothing from previous raids, turned his troops loose to sack the town. While his men were looting, burning, and drinking, Morgan himself organized and participated in robbing the Mount Sterling bank of eighty thousand dollars.

On June 11, the raiders entered Cynthiana and encountered a large contingent of Federal forces. Fighting viciously, Morgan's men defeated the Union soldiers and burned the town to the ground as the general confiscated money from local businessmen. Several more Confederate soldiers were killed, wounded, or captured, and Morgan's force dwindled to fewer than a thousand men.

Morgan led his victorious but battered force to a field just outside of Cynthiana and ordered a temporary camp set up to rest men and horses while he planned new strategy. The next morning, as the Rebels were just beginning to stir, five thousand Union cavalrymen swept onto the field, firing into the confused mass of Confederate soldiers. Caught unaware and unprepared, the Rebels fought halfheartedly, and within thirty minutes, dozens were killed and the remainder captured. During the short battle, Morgan and two enlisted men dug a shallow trench and buried the currency and bullion taken in the plunder of Mount Sterling and Cynthiana. Then Morgan and several men fled the scene of battle and, after several days' hard riding, reached Abingdon on June 24.

This last defeat at the hands of the Union forces ruined Morgan's reputation and career as a military man. He was now completely ignored by Confederate leaders. Several prominent generals called for his court martial for looting and extortion and requested an investigation into what became of all the gold, silver, and cash he had acquired during his raids and never turned over to the Southern treasury. A request for the eighty thousand dollars Morgan took from the Mount Sterling bank was drafted and delivered to the beleaguered general.

No one knows whether Morgan would have capitulated and returned any of his buried fortune, for he was killed during a Union attack on the Confederate headquarters at Greenville, South Carolina on September, 14, 1864.

If Morgan left maps or directions to the buried Civil War loot, they have never been found. At least a million dollars' worth of gold, silver, and currency is believed to have been cached in several places along routes Morgan traveled and at the battle site outside of Cynthiana, Kentucky. To date, not a penny of the treasure has been recovered.

Secret Silver Mine of the Cumberlands

The Cumberland Mountains of Tennessee have long puzzled geologists. Their research of the area strongly suggests that precious minerals are most unlikely to be found there. In spite of the scientists' qualified and authoritative declarations about the geology of the region, there are many persistent tales about the mining of silver deep these mountains.

The Cherokee Indians, who lived here long before the white man came, were known to have taken a fortune in silver from the Cumberland Mountains. One tale of treasure has a small party of Cherokee returning to the Piney Creek region of the range sometime in the late 1860s. The Indians, riding in two sturdy wagons pulled by mules, came from the Indian Territory (now Oklahoma) where they had been sent more than twenty years earlier. Before they left, the tribe elders had hidden their silver in the area and covered the entrances to their mines, planning to return someday for the fortune.

The small group of visiting Cherokee hid in the Piney Creek canyon during the day and left in the dark of night. Nearby residents who noticed the deep wheel ruts made by the departing wagons guessed that the vehicles carried a heavy load, and speculated that the Indians had recovered the tribe's hidden silver and taken it back to Oklahoma.

Attempts to backtrack the wagon trail to the secret mine failed.

One local intrigued by the tale of Indian silver mines in the Piney Creek area was a curious character named Leffew. Leffew lived with his wife and children deep in the wooded Cumberland Mountains not far from Piney Creek. He was a farmer, making a living for his family by growing corn and raising hogs and chickens on a hardscrabble mountaintop not far from Spring City.

Farmer Leffew was a tall, gaunt man with large hands calloused by years of hard outdoor work. His skin was leathery and tanned and always in need of washing. Those who chanced to visit the small Leffew farm in the woods remarked that it suffered badly from neglect.

Leffew's neighbors thought him peculiar, and most were uncomfortable around him. The rare times the farmer ventured into nearby settlements, he was generally avoided because of his ragged and unclean appearance. Leffew was often seen talking to himself, gesturing wildly, and sometimes screaming at demons only he could see. The old farmer also suffered from a severe nervous tic that caused his left shoulder to jerk sharply forward every few seconds, suggesting a grotesque dance and lending a bizarre touch to an already strange character.

Sometime early in the 1870s, Leffew began to neglect his farm and family more than usual, often disappearing for days at a time into the deep and gloomy canyons that spawned tributaries of Piney Creek. His frequent extended trips worried his wife and children.

One day Leffew arrived at the front door of his cabin and told his wife he had just discovered an old silver mine deep in Piney Creek gorge. From a dirty leather pouch that hung from his thin neck, he pulled a large nugget of almost pure silver and held it up as proof.

The next day, Leffew took his nugget into town and showed it to any who cared to see it. In a fit of behavior quite uncharacteristic for the eccentric old farmer, Leffew bought several rounds of drinks for everyone at a local tavern.

In a short time, Leffew, who normally drank not at all, began to feel the liquor. Proud of his new-found wealth, he boasted loudly of his secret mine. While bragging, Leffew let slip that the silver mine was in the Piney Creek gorge, not far from a prominent landmark known as Big Rock.

This announcement had an unwanted effect. Several men, coveting Leffew's silver, began searching for the mine. Leffew was followed each time he went into the woods, but being crafty in the wild, he eluded his trackers and vanished into the deep canyon of Piney Creek. For months, men tried to trail Leffew to his mine and always failed.

One afternoon, a young black man appeared at a mercantile in Evansville. He claimed Leffew had recently hired him to help dig the silver ore, and said Leffew had sent him to purchase some dynamite and mining supplies. The young man carefully loaded his purchases onto two mules and then led the pack animals out of town toward Piney Creek. It was the last time anyone ever saw him alive.

Several weeks later, his partially decomposed body was found on the bank of Piney Creek near where it joined one of its tributaries. The man had been shot through the head, and though few cared to say so too loudly or often, most believed Leffew had killed the young man to preserve the secret of the silver mine. To this day, the small canyon near where the body was found is known as Dead Negro Hollow.

In time, a rough-looking gang of men began to hang around the small Leffew farm. The farmer clearly disliked these desperate-looking characters and would caution his wife and children to remain in the cabin while he met with them out in the woods, beyond hearing. Though his wife asked him several times who they were, Leffew remained silent.

It soon leaked out, however, that the men were part of a gang of counterfeiters who allegedly minted phony silver coins in hiding deep in the mountains. Many townspeople suspected that Leffew had become part of the gang.

One afternoon after a brief, stormy meeting with several members of the gang at his farm, Leffew told his wife he was going to the mine and would be back the next day. After two days passed and her husband didn't come, Mrs. Leffew enlisted neighbors to help search for him. Another day went by, and the sheriff was called in. He organized yet another search, which was called off after a week when no trace of the farmer could be found.

About a year later, three young boys were hunting raccoons near Vinegar Hill when they made a grisly discovery. Hanging from the limb of a tree was the dried and shriveled body of a man. The corpse dangled from leather suspenders wrapped tightly around the victim's neck. The body had evidently been there for a long time, as the skin had dried around the skeleton. Clothing, boots, and other articles nearby suggested the skeleton had been Leffew.

Several years later, a local farmer named Thurmond, searching for stray cattle in the Piney Creek gorge, got lost. While climbing a steep wall of the canyon, he found an opening in the rock wide enough to allow the passage of a man. Several mounds of rock fragments outside the opening seemed to indicate that some excavation had taken place. Thurmond had heard of the secret mine of Farmer Leffew but never took it seriously. He wondered if he had accidentally discovered it.

Thurmond went on looking for his lost cattle, intending to some back another time and examine the opening in the rock more closely. Though he tried several times in later years to relocate the mysterious hole, he never could.

During the 1920s, a man named Warrick heard the story of the Leffew mine and decided to search for it. Warrick had lived in the region all his life, as had his father before him, and knew the country around Piney Creek. For months, Warrick spent several hours a day searching the Piney Creek gorge, always optimistic that he would eventually find the silver. Late one afternoon, the tired and begrimed Warrick arrived at his sister's home and announced to her he had discovered it!

Each day for several weeks thereafter, Warrick journeyed to the secret site near Piney Creek and excavated a small handful of silver ore. Each evening on his way home, he visited his sister and related the day's activities. Warrick's sister often asked to see some of the silver ore he had dug, but he steadfastly refused to show it to her. Finally, she accused Warrick of fabricating the story of his discovery.

One Sunday morning as Warrick and his sister were walking home from church, he told her he wanted to show her something important. He led her several yards off the trail near a place called Warrick Fork and showed her a large boulder. With some difficulty, Warrick rolled it to one side, revealing a shallow hole. Inside the hole were several leather pouches, each filled with nuggets of the purest silver.

Warrick explained to his sister that this was where he cached the silver dug from the mine. He told her that if anything ever happened to him, he wanted her to have his fortune.

Several more months passed, and Warrick continued to dig the silver from the secret mine and cache it beneath the large boulder. One morning, like so many other mornings, Warrick gathered his mining tools and headed out to Piney Creek. He cheerfully hailed his sister as he walked by her house on his way to his mine. It was the last time anyone ever saw Warrick.

To this day, no one knows whether Warrick met with foul play or simply decided to leave the country. After two weeks of fruitless searching, Warrick's sister and another relative went to the boulder to retrieve Warrick's cache. When the boulder was rolled aside, they found the shallow hole empty.

The Spring City region of the Cumberland Mountains in Tennessee is not much different today than it was when Leffew lived there in the late 1800s. Heavily forested and thinly populated, the region is infested with rattlesnakes and ticks, and moonshine stills are rumored to operate in the shallow caves and narrow canyons of the area.

In spite of the rugged and forbidding environment, occasional searchers for the secret silver mine of the Cumberland Mountains still come to this section of the Appalachians.

Tasso's Field of Confederate Gold

Tasso, Tennessee, lies just outside the western boundary of the Cherokee National Forest and about five miles northeast of the town of Cleveland in the Appalachian foothills. Scattered across a farmer's field by the railroad tracks just south of Tasso may lie Civil War relics and a fortune in gold and silver coins, the bizarre remains of a great explosion that disabled a Rebel train during the War Between the States.

The Cherokee Indians who originally settled this region called their small community Chatata, which means "clear water." When the Indians were removed in the early 1830s, white settlers took over their land. They retained the Cherokee name, and Chatata soon became a productive agricultural center in southeastern Tennessee. Around 1858, the railroad came through, connecting Chatata with the larger towns of Cleveland and Chattanooga to the southwest and Knoxville to the northeast.

During the Civil War, Chatata residents went about their business of planting, tending, and harvesting corn and other crops, trying to live as normally as they could under the circumstances. They saw hundreds of soldiers, both Union and Confederate, pass through and around their town, but for the most part, the small community was spared the misery of so many other settlements during that violent and bloody conflict.

The forces of both armies used the nearby railroad tracks, and it was not uncommon to see a Yankee troop train pass through in the morning and a Rebel one in the afternoon.

In the spring of 1864, Company C of the Confederate Army of Tennessee was camped by Chatata. The company had been ordered to scout the area and gauge the strength of any Union forces it encountered. If it could, the company was to attack and kill or capture any Yankees they found.

One morning, the commanding officer of Company C, a young captain, got word that a Union troop train was approaching from the southwest. The train was said to carry two hundred soldiers, a supply of guns and ammunition, and three cannons. The officer decided to try to wreck the train and get the weapons.

He also learned that the Union train was being pursued by a Confederate train. The Rebel train consisted of a locomotive and five cars. Most carried men and horses, but the second car behind the locomotive held a large payroll in gold and silver coins destined for a Confederate camp about ten miles up the line at Charleston. The payroll car also held guns, ammunition, sabers, and other military equipment.

The two trains were close enough to exchange gunfire as they traveled, and at least one Yankee was killed.

The commanding officer summoned Private Isaac Griffith and ordered him to set an explosive charge the Union train would detonate as it passed over. Once the train was disabled, the mounted Rebels were to swoop down on the scene and kill or capture any surviving Yankees. To spare Chatata any damage, Private Griffith was told to set the charge several hundred yards south of the town.

Pressed for time, Griffith hurriedly attached the explosives to the railroad bed at the designated point. Once satisfied with the placement of the charge, Griffith leaped onto his mount and sped to his fellows, who had gathered on a low hill nearby to await the train.

Moments later, the mounted Rebs heard the trains approaching and the guns firing. As the Union locomotive came into view, a huge cheer rose from the expectant troops. Their cheering turned into horrified silence as the Union train passed over the charges without setting them off. As it roared on away, the Confederate locomotive smashed into the charge, generating a gigantic explosion that destroyed the engine and the next two cars. The rest of the train jumped the tracks.

When the smoke cleared, the stunned Rebels saw pieces of the train, military equipment, and fellow soldiers scattered several dozen yards on either side of the railroad tracks. The payroll had been transported in canvas sacks piled within a wooden crate. The crate was blown to bits by the explosion, and coins were hurled across the surrounding countryside.

The screams and groans of the wounded and dying reached the ears of the mounted Rebels, who quickly mobilized. As the company advanced to aid their stricken comrades, they were suddenly attacked by a large Yankee force that charged out of the nearby woods. The Confederates, completely unprepared for the onslaught, fled for their lives, unmindful of orders barked by their frantic captain.

Several Rebels were killed or wounded as they raced across the fields, but most of them escaped into the woods. A few were taken prisoner.

The Union troops, ignorant of the gold payroll, glanced over the accident scene and quickly abandoned the area.

Attracted by the sound of the explosion and the initial billow of dark smoke, Chatata residents ran to the scene and gave what help they could to the surviving Confederate soldiers. The gold and silver coins and military supplies lay unnoticed in the nearby fields.

With the passing of generations, the accidental demolition of the Confederate train faded from the memories of area residents and soon became only a minor footnote in the history of the region. After the Civil War, Chatata grew and prospered and became one of several pleasant and attractive communities in the scenic foothills on the western side of the Appalachian Mountains.

In 1905, residents of Chatata changed the name of the town to Tasso. The name was that of an Italian gentleman who often rode the train through the small town. When the train stopped to let off and take on passengers, Tasso would stand on the rear deck of the caboose and sing opera to any who cared to listen. The townspeople often gathered in large crowds to hear him. They must have loved his singing.

In 1970, the destroyed Confederate train was brought back into people's awareness by a Tasso youth's remarkable discovery. On a hot afternoon with locusts whirring in the trees, sixteen-year-old Ben Casteel was playing along Chatata Creek where it runs parallel with the railroad tracks for several yards. He noticed something slightly out of place in the muddy bottom of the shallow stream and investigated. To his surprise, he pulled a Confederate saber from the thick mud. Though rusted and dirty, the saber was in good condition. Upon examination, it was determined to be part of the shipment of military goods carried in the blown-up train. The discovery of the saber revived the story, and people soon were searching the area for more of the relics—and for the gold and silver coins.

Since the saber, many other relics have been found: mess kits, silverware, parts of boots, brass buttons, and belt buckles. No coins have been found, but a researcher who has examined the site has an explanation. He also claims to know where to find the coins.

Gold and silver, he says, are relatively heavy metals. When coins lie on soft and often muddy soil, as at this site, they gradually sink below the surface. The area near the railroad tracks is also flooded once or twice each year. When the ground is saturated with water, the individual soil grains separate easily, permitting any dense object to sink. The local flooding is also believed to have added at least two and perhaps as much as four feet of silt to the field since the explosion well over a hundred years ago.

The individual gold and silver coins, the expert says, are probably between five and ten feet below the surface.

Locating the coins would mean removing a considerable amount of topsoil, an idea not encouraged by local farmers. One enterprising treasure hunter has suggested a series of narrow trenches to be dug one at a time near the explosion. Each trench would be excavated to ten feet and the unearthed soil carefully examined with metal detectors. The trench would then be refilled and another dug, causing minimum disruption and damage.

If it could be agreed to by all concerned, this method might yield a bountiful harvest of gold and silver coins and Confederate Army relics.

Buried Union Army Payroll

In the spring of 1902, the town of Rogersville, Tennessee had just survived the worst storm to strike the area in a decade. High winds had destroyed several homes, and removed shingles and toppled chimneys from others. Crops were ruined, and huge trees had blown down, with their broken and torn roots splayed out like so many spider legs.

Several days after the storm, three boys were hunting rabbits through the debris. At a deadfall, one of the boys, Bobby Venable, saw a hole where a large tree root had been pulled out. Hoping to grab a rabbit, the boy knelt at the hole and thrust his arm inside. His fingers touched pieces of cold metal! The youth pulled one out and was surprised and excited to discover it was a silver coin. In fact, the hole was full of coins, all U.S. silver dollars.

The three boys enlarged the hole and found a metal cooking pot partially filled with the coins. The pot had evidently been tipped over when the roots were pulled from the ground, spilling some of the coins.

The boys filled their pockets and game bags with the coins and went home, intending to keep the discovery secret. Their parents soon found out, though, and encouraged the youths to turn the coins over to authorities and let them try to find the rightful owner. The silver dollars had a face value of $1,512.

It was not clear who owned the land on which the coins were found, and an investigation lasted weeks.

Meanwhile, several newspapers reported the discovery, and the news spread nationwide.

Bobby Venable received a letter with a New York postmark from an elderly man who had read about the discovery. The writer, who had served in Tennessee in the Union army during the Civil War, told how the coins came to be buried there.

Sometime in 1864, he was promoted to corporal and assigned to a Union escort carrying a huge payroll in silver coins for four hundred troops stationed near the Tennessee–North Carolina border. As the escort approached Big Creek near Rogersville, it was attacked by a company of Confederate troops.

Badly outnumbered, the Union escort retreated into the nearby woods, looking for a place to turn and fight. Once inside a perimeter of trees, the officer in charge ordered his men to dismount and return fire. For several hours, firing from behind tree trunks and fallen logs, the Yankees held off the attacking Rebels. But as the Union soldiers fell one by one to Confederate bullets, the outcome became clear.

Not wanting the payroll to fall into enemy hands, the commanding officer enlisted one of his men to help him hide the silver. That man was the corporal who wrote young Bob Venable thirty-eight years later.

The officer and the corporal unloaded payroll sacks and other supplies from the mules and went from tree to tree digging shallow holes. Into each, they put two or three of the canvas sacks and a few supply items, until all of it was hidden. The former corporal recalled digging one hole large enough to hold a cooking pot. He put several sacks of coins into it and hastily refilled the hole. Once the payroll and supplies were hidden, the officer told the corporal they would return for the cache if they survived the attack.

Minutes after returning to the fight, the officer took a bullet through the head and died. Only a handful of Union soldiers remained alive, and the corporal fled into the woods, far from the sounds of combat.

The writer said he wandered days, finding neither food nor water, before happening on an isolated farm. The farmer and his wife took him in, fed him, and gave him a new set of clothes. Having had his fill of the war, the corporal went home to New York, where he lived in hiding for many years because he was a deserter.

He wrote that he and the officer buried portions of the payroll silver in at least a dozen different locations, always at the base of large trees.

Venable first shared this letter with his two friends, and then made it public. Hundreds of treasure hunters came to Rogersville to dig for the hidden payroll. Soon the forest near Big Creek looked like a shelled battlefield because of the many small excavations.

Near the original find, several relics were discovered, no doubt remnants of the battle: bridle bits, tools, a stirrup, and several buttons from both Yankee and Rebel uniforms.

None of the remaining payroll silver was ever found.

After several weeks, the tide of treasure hunters began to ebb and Rogersville gradually returned to normal. Nothing more was heard from the former Union corporal, and the incident was forgotten.

Perhaps another severe storm will one day strike the Rogersville area, blowing shingles from the roofs and felling large trees in the forest. Perhaps another cache of silver dollars will be discovered and the search renewed.

The Cave of Gold Above Elk River

The more remote parts of the Tennessee Appalachians are rugged and almost impenetrable, made up of deep, dark hollows, steep ridges, and infinite treacherous caves. Natural hazards such a rattlesnakes, cottonmouths, ticks, and poison ivy abound in the wild region. Rumor says there are whiskey stills in the deep recesses of the mountain range, but most residents don't want to talk about that.

Isolated parts of the range are overgrown with dense thickets of briars and tangled undergrowth. It is easy to get lost in there, and once lost, hard to be found.

Somewhere in this forbidding environment, a great Spanish treasure was reportedly left more than four hundred years ago—a treasure of hundreds of golden ingots and artifacts that required twenty mules and an armed escort to transport. It is a treasure hoard that to this day remains hidden in the Tennessee Appalachians.

As rugged and dangerous as parts of these mountains are today, they were even more so before the plows and axes of white settlers cleared the hillsides and lowlands for corn and other crops more than a hundred years ago. In time, much of the region was tamed and settled.

One afternoon in 1886, an old Cherokee arrived at the small community of Pelham. He was dirty, disheveled, and road-weary, and apparently hadn't had a solid meal in weeks. His clothes were torn and the soles of his pitiful shoes had long since worn through. The old man said he had walked all the way from the Cherokee Reservation in eastern Oklahoma.

Going from house to house and farm to farm, the Indian offered to trade work for food. Two days later, a local farmer hired him to chop wood and do other chores. The old Indian proved a hard and efficient worker who labored from dawn until far past sundown. He never seemed to tire and seldom stopped except to get a drink of water. The old Cherokee slept in the farmer's barn.

During the two weeks he labored on the small farm, the farmer and the Cherokee came to know one another, and one evening over dinner, the Indian explained why he had come to eastern Tennessee.

In halting and clumsy English, the Indian said that many of the older Cherokee in Oklahoma knew of a hidden Spanish treasure near the "hills of Mannanetcha," the divide between the Elk and Duck Rivers.

Many generations earlier, the Indian said, a Spanish mule train was attempting a particularly broken and difficult part of the mountain range when it was set upon by Cherokee.

The Indians attacked early one morning, when the pack mules had been loaded and the Spaniards were getting breakfast. The escort was caught by surprise and killed within minutes.

When the Cherokee ransacked the mule packs, they found gold—in the form of hundreds of ingots, several sacks of coins, and other items such as chalices and candleholders. Since the Cherokee sometimes used gold to make ornaments, they stored the treasure in a nearby cave.

In succeeding years, the Cherokee periodically visited the cave to retrieve gold for making bracelets, necklaces and ceremonial jewelry, but by and large the treasure remained intact.

The old Cherokee who had come to Pelham said he carried directions to the cave in which the treasure was stored, but refused to show them. He did say that the golden hoard was hidden in a limestone cave somewhere on a steep mountainside in the area. The cave had a very low opening, and even from only a few yards away, was difficult to see. According to the directions, a freshwater spring issued from the mouth of the cave, cascading down the mountainside to the Elk River below.

The Indian said the entrance to the cave was probably covered thickly with forest vegetation and would be hard to locate. He planned to find the stream where it met the Elk River and follow it up the side of the mountain to its source.

Near the entrance of the cave, the Indian said, a cross was carved into an exposed rock. When the Cherokee attacked the hapless mule train, they had noticed the symbol of the cross embossed on weapons, armor, and saddlebags, he said. After they hid the gold, they copied the symbol onto a nearby rock to mark the cave's entrance.

As the story of hidden treasure spread through the area, several neighbors offered to help the old Indian in his search. He refused them all.

After two weeks of recuperation from his long journey, the Cherokee had regained much of his strength. He bid his employer goodbye and went into the nearby mountains.

A Pelham resident spotted the old Indian leaving and decided to follow him. The man had been intrigued by the story of the hidden Spanish treasure and thought of searching for it himself. He followed the Cherokee into the Elk River canyon, but there lost him after only a few hundred yards.

For several days, no one saw the Indian. Then he reappeared, but he carried no treasure. He said he had followed several small springs to their sources on the mountainside, but none of them issued from the treasure cave.

After resting a few more days, the Indian left once more for the Elk River valley. He was never seen again. Some speculated that the old man had found the treasure and departed, his pockets filled with riches. Others suggested he failed in his search and went back to Oklahoma. Still others thought the old man might have perished, alone in the harsh mountains.

Intrigued by the old Indian's tale, several locals tried to find the treasure cave over the next few years. In 1893, a group of searchers found a rock near the Elk River chiseled with a large cross. The carving was quite weathered, as if it had been made hundreds of years earlier. The discovery of the cross renewed interest in the hidden gold, and soon the hills and canyons were alive with treasure hunters.

The cave was never found.

Where there are caves in the Appalachians, the mountains are normally made of thinly bedded, highly jointed, and porous limestone rock. This kind of rock is easily eroded by percolating ground water that seeps down through it. Sometimes ground water is trapped in the limestone aquifer for centuries and eventually drawn back to the surface through wells. Sometimes the water may flow for hundreds of miles deep below the surface as an underground river. Occasionally this stored ground water escapes to the surface as a spring.

Earthquakes and occasional shifts in weakened and aged rock formations can change the course of the underground water, cutting off springs in some areas and starting others elsewhere.

Given the geology of the Tennessee Appalachians, the spring of which the old Cherokee spoke may no longer flow from the treasure cave as it did over four hundred years ago.

The low entrance to the treasure cave probably still looks out across Elk River valley, though. Thick foliage and dense undergrowth may have made the entrance hard to find, and hunters and outdoorsmen may have passed close to it over the centuries and never noticed it, but just inside this small cave in the Mannanetcha Hills may still lie a vast fortune in Spanish gold ingots and artifacts.

South Carolina & North Carolina

NORTH CAROLINA

1. The Bechtler Gold Coins
2. Twenty Mule Loads of Silver
3. Pots of Confederate Gold
4. The Cursed Cache of the Uwharrie Mountains
5. Outlaw Treasure Cave Near Hendersonville

SOUTH CAROLINA

6. Lost Keg of Gold
7. The Indian Gold Mine de Soto Never Found
8. Silver Mine in Pickens County

The Bechtler Gold Coins

Between 1831 and 1840, a small, privately-owned mint operated in the remote town of Rutherfordton. Its owners mined, processed, and coined nearly forty million dollars' worth of gold over a nine-year period. The coins, cast into denominations of $1.00, $2.50, and $5.00, were in general circulation in western North Carolina, northern South Carolina, and much of northern Georgia.

As United States-minted specie became available, these locally made coins were gradually withdrawn from the area economy. Collectors now possess hundreds, perhaps thousands, of the coins, and many more of them, perhaps millions of dollars' worth, are still in Rutherford County. So is the rich mine from which the gold came.

Few are aware of it, but most of the gold mined in the United States between 1790 and 1840 came from western North Carolina and parts of South Carolina and Georgia. North Carolina supplied most of the gold coined by the U.S. mint in Philadelphia during that period, and according to a 1948 U.S. Geological Survey report, there were about three hundred gold-producing mines in North Carolina alone. Rutherfordton, in the western part of the state about forty miles southeast of Asheville, was known as America's gold mining capitol during the early 1800s.

Although most of the gold used for minting U.S. coins came from western North Carolina, U.S. money was, in fact, quite scarce in the region. Because of that, some area residents made their own from locally mined gold. These maverick coins were in common use throughout the region and were generally accepted.

In 1830, a German immigrant named Christopher Bechtler and his son, August, arrived in the small community of Rutherfordton. The Bechtlers had been metallurgists and jewelers in Europe, and they hoped to put their skills to use in the famous gold fields of the Carolinas.

The Bechtlers found a promising outcrop in Rutherford County near Rutherfordton, settled, and soon discovered a rich deposit of gold-bearing quartz on their new land. As they mined the ore, the Bechtlers decided to open their own mint. They built a roller and a stamp press, and began producing a high quality specie in denominations of $1.00, $2.50, and $5.00. Area residents came to prefer the Bechtler coins, and they began to be used almost exclusively throughout the region.

The Bechtlers preferred minting their own coins to selling raw and smelted gold to the Philadelphia mint. Hauling the heavy ore from western North Carolina to eastern Pennsylvania was a long and arduous journey and took time that could have been spent digging gold. Robbers occasionally lurked along the old ore trail, and more than one hauler was killed for his rich load. Selling the gold to a broker or middleman meant reduced profit. Thus, Christopher and August Bechtler decided to optimize their profit by continuing to fashion their own gold into what came to be known as "Bechtler coins." They also charged a small fee to mint the gold brought in by other area miners. In a few years, the two men became very wealthy.

For nine years the Bechtler mine and mint prospered. It has been estimated that forty million dollars' worth of coins (at today's market value) were made. Most of them went into the area economy.

But the Bechtler mint was not destined to endure. In 1840, the United States opened a mint in Charlotte, about seventy-five miles east of Rutherfordton. With U.S.–minted specie now more available in the region, the Bechtlers were pressured by the federal government to cease their private manufacture of coins. The family didn't object, since by that time it had already amassed a fortune. Western North Carolinians, however, often insisted on using the Bechtler coins. They were preferred by most area merchants and residents, and for well over twenty years, the coins were the most common form of currency in this part of the Appalachians.

During the War Between The States, Bechtler coins were also in demand by the Confederate government. One historian noted that Confederate purchasing contracts often specifically called for payment in Bechtler gold rather than U.S. gold or paper money. Metallurgical analysis showed that the Bechtler coins had a higher gold content than did the U.S.minted coins! They were also more plentiful in the area and more acceptable to merchants and suppliers who had been happily using them for years.

As the Civil War raged, even after North Carolina joined the Confederacy, the western section of the state was spared much of the violence that disrupted the rest of the South. Though most of the conflict occurred elsewhere, many families in and near the Carolina Appalachians buried large caches of Bechtler coins so they would not be confiscated by roving bands of either Yankee soldiers or Rebel bandits who terrorized the countryside.

Within months after closing down his mine, Christopher Bechtler, along with a trunk filled with gold coins, disappeared. He was traveling by wagon to nearby Buncombe County to pay off a large debt. He was last seen at the Parris Gap toll gate, where he stopped to visit with the operator for about an hour. A few days later, Bechtler's wagon was found overturned in a deep ravine about three miles west of the gap. His two horses had been killed and their carcasses lay near the ruined wagon. Christopher Bechtler and the trunk of coins were never seen again.

His son August closed down the mine shortly thereafter. August abandoned the settlement near the mine and moved into Rutherfordton, where he opened a shop and made jewelry, firearms, and occasionally, in response to local demand, a few coins, using some of the original rollers and dies. Beset with serious health problems, August Bechtler passed away a few years later, leaving his business and his fortune to his closest relative, a cousin who had come to live with him five years earlier. The cousin, also named Christopher and sometimes referred to in the region as Christopher Junior, ran the business for several years. Then he closed it down and moved away, not saying where he was bound.

The Bechtler coins gradually disappeared from circulation over the years, to be replaced by federal specie. As the coins became a part of the region's history, the Smithsonian Institution saw fit to create a display of them. Coin collectors considered them valuable both intrinsically and as historical artifacts. Researchers have recently learned that several current Rutherfordton residents still hold hundreds, perhaps even thousands, of the Bechtler coins. Interviews have revealed that many of the town's citizens own several hundred of the old coins, which were handed down in their families. These collections of Bechtler coins could be worth from several hundred thousands to well over a million dollars on today's collector market.

The Bechtler coins still turn up from time to time. One long-time Rutherfordton resident reported finding hundreds of the coins in a secret hiding place in the concrete-lined chimney of an old house that Christopher Bechtler had lived in. The coins were picked out of a square, hollow cement chamber. It has also been suggested that many coins hidden during the Civil War were never retrieved and still lie buried in the area.

Some of the minting equipment once used by the Bechtlers is still around. The rollers and the stamp press, both valuable artifacts, are held by local residents. The original dies used in the manufacture of the coins served as door stops for a Rutherfordton family for twenty years. When World War II broke out, the lady of the house donated them to the government during a scrap-metal drive!

The location of the original Bechtler mine, with its rich, seemingly inexhaustible supply of almost pure gold, was well known for generations. When Christopher Bechtler closed it down in 1840, the vein of gold was reported to be as rich and abundant as the day it was discovered. August reopened the mine for a brief time during the mid–1840s, then shut it down for good.

Around the turn of the century, the open shaft, regarded as a hazard, was covered over and fenced off. Over the years, the town's residents largely forgot the mine, using it as a garbage dump.

One Rutherfordton old-timer actually entered the mine around 1945. He claimed he and his father were lowered into the shaft on a rope, and once inside they walked around the excavation for several minutes, discovering artifacts, furniture, and mining apparatus. The old-timer recalled that the air in the mine was bad and smelled strongly of gas. He also reported the shaft was almost knee-deep in water that was seeping in through the fractured rock. He and his father left quickly, and to his knowledge, no one has gone down the old shaft since.

Today, the old Bechtler mine is a victim of progress. Contruction projects and real estate developments have covered the area where it was believed to have been, completely cutting off access to the rich ore that lies below the ground.

Rutherfordton is today a pleasant community attractively sprawled in the shadows of the Carolina Appalachians. It's a typical small American town, and few that walk the streets and travel the highways of this village of some thirty-five hundred souls know that it was once a place where fortunes in gold were mined and minted.

Twenty Mule-Loads of Silver

In far western North Carolina near the Nantahala Gorge, fast-flowing rivers and streams have carved impressive canyons into the fractured, folded, and uplifted rock that makes up this portion of the Appalachian Mountains. It was there, one day in 1896, that an aged Cherokee Indian inadvertently revealed to a young white boy the existence of a long-hidden secret cache of twenty mule-loads of silver somewhere near Silver Creek.

The young boy was W.I. Grant, born in a small log cabin alongside Wesser Creek in 1881. Grant's father raised corn and hogs on the narrow bottomland by the creek and made a fair living during a time that was hard on most people in the area. With several children, the Grants had little food to spare, and many a meal was postponed. Regardless, the family never turned a hungry traveler from the door.

One day in 1893, a trader arrived in the region of Wesser Creek with a wagonload of goods. The Grant family had no money to make purchases, but they did feed a meal to the merchant and his Indian helper. At first, the old Indian stayed in the yard, not realizing he was welcome in the home of white people, but Mrs. Grant called him inside and invited him to sit at the table and dine with the rest of the family. Though not plentiful, the food was delicious, and the Grants were happy to share their slim fare with their guests.

As the trader and Grant's father caught up on the news of the day, the youngster, W.I., devoted all his attention to the Indian, and the Indian seemed pleased by the child's interest.

The Indian told young Grant that he was called Bigfoot and was a member of the Cherokee tribe. Bigfoot was large for an Indian, towering nearly six-and-a-half feet. He was about fifty, well-muscled and strong, and always carried a big rifle. His feet were the obvious source of his name.

After the meal, the trader thanked the Grants, left a few goods and trinkets in appreciation, and he and Bigfoot rode away in the wagon.

Several days later, the huge Indian appeared at the front door of the Grant cabin. He presented a dressed deer carcass to Mrs. Grant, and told her the deer was a token of his gratitude for the meal and the hospitality given him on his earlier visit. With a slight bow, he excused himself and disappeared into the nearby woods. Bigfoot seemed to know the Grants had barely enough food to feed their large family and that the shared meal must have taxed their meager resources.

About a week later, young Grant was working in the cornfield with his father when he saw Bigfoot approach, carrying several wild geese by their necks. He handed the cleaned fowl to the older Grant and merely said, "Food." With a smile and a nod, he turned and once again retreated into the forest.

Bigfoot made several more sudden and quiet appearances, bringing gifts of deer, geese, grouse, and sometimes fish. The Grants always thanked him for the food and began to ask the Indian to dine with them each time he came.

One evening, Bigfoot told the Grants he had left the trader because he preferred to live in the woods instead of getting by like a white man. The Grants told the big Indian he was welcome on their farm any time, and Bigfoot soon became a regular visitor, always bringing food and occasionally toys he had carved for the children. He played with all the youngsters, but W.I. was his favorite.

Young W.I. Grant was fascinated by Bigfoot's huge rifle, and he would often run his hand over the smooth, shiny barrel and poke his finger into the bore. Bigfoot told the lad that when he was older and stronger, he would show him how to shoot the gun, and as the boy grew, the two spent much time together in the woods. Bigfoot taught Grant to read animal sign, set traps for small game, and find the finest herbs and greens in the forest. Bigfoot continued his regular visits to the Grant farm over the years and became almost a part of the family.

One day, Bigfoot and the boy were sunning themselves on a large rock overlooking Wesser Creek. They had caught some fish, and as the afternoon wore on, the two relaxed, enjoying the late summer weather. While young Grant reclined on the rock, Bigfoot molded bullets for his rifle, heating the metal over a small flame and pressing it into shape using a hand-forged tool he always carried.

Bigfoot looked thoughtfully around at the canyon, the woods, and the sky, and with a deep sigh told the boy that one day all the deer, geese, and fish would be gone. He added that the Indians would someday be gone as well.

Worried, Grant asked what he meant. Bigfoot explained that the area was rapidly filling up with white men, and that when white men arrive, all the game and the Indians are killed off or run out.

When Grant asked why, Bigfoot replied that white men were greedy, wanting most of all the silver that was found in these hills. He showed young Grant the bullets he was molding and told him they were not made from lead, but from pure silver.

The lad asked where the silver came from, and Bigfoot pointed to a nearby ridge. The Cherokee had had a secret silver mine for hundreds of years, he said, in the mountains on the other side of the ridge near Silver Creek. He said the mine was rich with the precious metal, but when white men started moving into the area, the Cherokee closed it down, knowing the white man's unbridled greed for such things. When the boy asked for more details, Bigfoot cut him off sharply and told him it was forbidden for members of the tribe even to talk about the silver.

When he finished making his bullets, the Indian handed several to Grant and told him to keep them hidden and bring them out only when he was a grown man and he, Bigfoot, was no longer around.

About a week after Bigfoot had described the secret silver mine of the Cherokees, young Grant, then fifteen, walked to Silver Creek and climbed over and through the ravines and hillsides in search of the mine. He found nothing that remotely resembled a mine, but he did discover two primitive smelters that had obviously gone unused for many years. Grant knew he was in the right area and rightly guessed that the Cherokee used the smelters to process their ore. The youngster was determined to quiz Bigfoot about the silver mine on his next visit.

When Bigfoot came the next week, he was drunk and still sipping from a half-full jar of strong homemade whiskey. He and young Grant went into the woods and laid down beneath a large tree. As Bigfoot grew more and more inebriated, Grant took advantage of his state and asked pointed questions about the silver mine.

Presently, Bigfoot began to laugh and talk incoherently about the trick the Cherokee had played on the white man. When Grant asked him what he meant, the Indian told an intriguing tale.

Many years ago, he said, white men had heard about the silver mine of the Cherokee and came to the Silver Creek valley in search of it. Like Grant, all they found were the remains of the old smelters. The Cherokee, according to Bigfoot, took all the silver from the mine and secreted it inside a large hollowed-out rock some distance away.

For many days and nights, the Indians worked in the mine, digging out the silver and smelting it with their crude equipment. Bigfoot said they dug twenty mule-loads of the ore before moving it. While many Indians dug the silver, several others hollowed out an opening in a boulder large enough to hold all of the silver. Once the bags of ore were placed in the hollow boulder, a large slab of the same kind of rock was placed over the opening.

The Indians swore to each other to keep secret the true story of the silver and to punish by death any violation of the oath. They let the white men believe they had merely covered the mine, leaving the silver inside, and let them search for it. Over the years, Cherokees who knew of the treasure-filled boulder would occasionally retrieve some ore to make bullets and jewelry.

When Grant asked Bigfoot where the hollowed-out rock was, the drunken Cherokee pulled an old, weathered, grimy deerskin map from his pocket and handed it to the youth. The map contained Indian symbols, and though it was hard to read, Grant could make out some familiar landmarks. While the boy was reading the map, the big Indian fell asleep in a stupor.

For nearly two hours Grant studied the map, memorizing the marked trails, mountain peaks, ridges, and streams. Presently, the Indian awoke and saw the boy holding the map. Bigfoot asked Grant if he had told him the story of the hidden Cherokee silver. The boy replied that he had, and handed the map back to him.

Bigfoot held out an open palm and told the boy to keep the map. He said he had broken a tribal code by revealing the information and would likely be killed for it. He told Grant to hide the map and never let anyone know he possessed it, or he, too, would be killed. The boy promised to hide the map and keep the secret.

Bigfoot bid the lad goodbye and staggered into the woods. Two weeks later, his body was found about a mile from the Grant cabin. The big Indian's throat had been cut from ear to ear, and a knife had been thrust into his chest up to the hilt.

The death of Bigfoot had a devastating effect on young Grant. Because he and the Indian had been close friends, the boy grieved for many weeks, but the resilience of youth finally won out, and life returned to normal. True to his promise, Grant told no one about the treasure map and kept it hidden.

Many years later when Grant was grown, he dug the map out of its hiding place and undertook a search for the silver cache. Following the directions on the old, cracked deerskin, Grant went right to the boulder, lifted the covering rock, and saw the many leather sacks filled with silver lying in the hollowed-out chamber. Grant spent an entire afternoon sitting on top of the boulder wondering what to do with this vast fortune. In the end, he covered it up and left it where it was.

Years later, when asked how he could walk away from such a great wealth, he replied without hesitation that it was simply not his treasure. It belonged to the Cherokee, he said. They mined it, they labored hard and long to move it to the hollowed-out rock, and they guarded it over the years. At first, he said, he was afraid the Indians would somehow find out if he removed some of the silver and he would die a horrible death like his friend Bigfoot, but in the end, he believed it was simply not rightfully his to take.

The map, Grant said, was in an old trunk filled with belongings, and he intended to leave it there.

In the fall of 1954, W.I. Grant passed away at age seventy-three. A friend of Grant's who knew the story of the Cherokee silver asked his widow about the map. She had no idea where it was. When the friend told her Grant had said he kept it in an old trunk, she explained apologetically that the trunk and everything in it had been burned right after the funeral.

Unless some Cherokee still live who remember, the secret of the great cache of silver somewhere on Silver Creek near the Nantahala Gorge died with W.I. Grant. Many remember there was a silver mine, but few know that the great wealth of precious metal was removed and hidden in a huge hollowed-out boulder. Most of that twenty muleloads of almost pure silver is still there.

Pots of Confederate Gold

Toward the end of 1864 it was becoming painfully clear to the Confederate Army that the war was winding down and they were losing. Some Southern generals, foreseeing the inevitable outcome, came to be more interested in salvaging what was left of the Confederate treasury than in winning battles. To that end, much of the Southern army's wealth, intended to purchase arms, ammunition, and riding stock, was hurriedly hidden in various places below the Mason-Dixon Line. Some of this wealth was later retrieved, but most of it, perhaps several million dollars' worth of gold and silver coins, remains hidden.

One such cache was an incredibly rich store of gold held in a temporary treasury headquarters in Richmond, Virginia, during the war. When it became clear that the days of the Confederacy were numbered, military leaders decided to hide the gold so it would not fall into the hands of Union forces. Captain J.W. Duchase, commander of Company C of the Fourth Mississippi Infantry stationed in Richmond, was charged with removing the South's store of gold coins to another state and burying them in predetermined locations.

Duchase was roused from his sleep around two o'clock one crisp autumn morning in 1864 and told to report to headquarters. There he found officers and aides frantically preparing to abandon the area in the wake of the news that the Yankees were closing in.

Duchase, along with his entire company, was ordered to report to the railway station at 6:30 that evening. Each man was to bring three days' worth of rations, at least forty rounds of ammunition, and full marching gear.

That evening, Captan Duchase and the seventy-eight fighting men from Mississippi who made up his infantry company assembled at the station platform. The train had four boxcars and three flatcars. The boxcars contained arms, ammunition, and other material the Confederate leaders thought prudent to ship out. The end flatcar held a three-inch-bore fieldpiece, some other armament, and a detachment of gunners. The two remaining flatcars were loaded with iron cooking pots, each filled with gold coins, each lid tightly fastened with wire.

As Duchase waited near the train, he was delivered a set of orders and told to open them when he arrived at his assigned destination, Greensboro, North Carolina.

Duchase's notes on the incident explain what occurred next:

> We traveled all night and reached Greensboro the next day at 4 P.M. There I opened my orders and found the following instructions: 'You are to proceed the following night to McLeansville by way of the North Carolina Railroad. After leaving McLeansville, you will bury these pots in groups of three on each side of the R.R. and not over one hundred paces from the right of way. In case there are houses nearby, proceed further. Also, plot the burial places as nearly as possible.'

Duchase and his men followed the orders to the letter, burying the pots in lots of three. In all, they covered about sixteen miles along the railroad tracks between Greensboro and Company Shops (later renamed Burlington).

Their mission complete, Duchase and his infantry company rode the train into Company Shops, turned the train around, and returned to Greensboro. From Greensboro, they went by another train toward Richmond to submit the information on the locations of the buried

Confederate gold and to aid in the defense of that city against Yankee attack. Along the way, however, the train was derailed by a Union blockade, and most of Company C was captured. Duchase and one lieutenant escaped, but they lost the description of the burial locations in doing so.

The two men lived in hiding for several weeks and were forced to steal and beg food from the isolated farms they found in the area. Union troops eventually found Duchase and his companion. The two men, near starvation, were huddling under a fallen log. They surrendered to the Yankees, were interrogated, and waited out the remainder of the war in a prison camp.

When the South surrendered, Duchase, along with thousands of other captured Rebels, was freed. He went to Mexico and got involved in mining and real estate. He prospered over the years from several successful ventures, married a Mexican woman, and raised a family. Duchase sometimes thought of returning to North Carolina for the Confederate gold he had buried. The former infantry captain believed he remembered enough of the area between Greensboro and McLeansville to locate the treasure easily. Business concerns and family matters, however, occupied his time, and he could not travel. While living in Mexico, Duchase wrote extensive notes in a journal about the war in general and his assignment to conceal the Confederate gold in particular. His descriptions of where he hid the gold-filled iron cooking pots were clear and precise.

More years passed. Duchase's wealth grew, and his desire to return to the United States waned. His notes on the war, along with the account of the buried Confederate gold, were given to a man named P.H. Black, a former Greensboro resident who met Duchase in Mexico in the 1890s. When Duchase learned Black was from North Carolina, he told him the story. Before Black left Mexico, Duchase gave him all his notes about it.

Duchase died in Mexico around the turn of the century, having never left since he first arrived in 1865. P.H.

Black died in North Carolina in the 1930s, and no one knows what became of Duchase's notes. Nor does anyone know whether Black ever tried to retrieve any of the gold. If he did, he did not find all of it.

During the 1880s, Burlington grew into an important settlement in that part of the Appalachian piedmont. In the fields and meadows along the old North Carolina Railroad tracks, farmers met the growing demand for cotton and corn.

Late one summer afternoon in 1910, a black farmhand was plowing in a field about three miles west of Burlington. The horse-drawn plowing was tedious and the day was hot. Both man and horse were tired and looking forward to quitting time when the steel plow struck something hard, breaking its point. The farmhand dug into the ground and retrieved a rusted iron cooking pot wrapped tightly with thick wire. He wrestled the heavy pot to the surface, and when he removed the wire and the lid, he was surprised to find it filled to the top with twenty-dollar gold pieces. The farmhand was about a hundred paces from the old railroad tracks.

Not knowing the true value of the coins, the farmhand took several into Burlington the next day and traded them for dimes. The twenty-dollar gold pieces aroused local curiosity, and the laborer was asked about his discovery. Before sundown of that same day, the corn field was swarming with men digging the rich soil for other pots. Within two feet of the first iron pot, the landowner found two others. Though he never told anyone the value of his discovery, from that day on he was a wealthy man.

The three pots of gold were found in the corn field by luck and accident. Others may have been recovered, but if so it has never been recorded. Most likely, hundreds of the iron cooking pots, each filled with gold coins, are still buried near the old railroad tracks. For well over a hundred twenty years, a king's ransom has lain hidden in the fields under a few inches of North Carolina soil.

The Cursed Cache of the Uwharrie Mountains

In west-central North Carolina about fifty miles south of Greensboro lie the Uwharrie Mountains, an ancient subdivision of the Appalachians. Geologists have written that the Uwharries might be the oldest range on the North American continent and at one time reached altitudes surpassing any found today in the Rockies.

Because of their great age, the Uwharries have eroded over time, the once-majestic peaks now worn down into no more than rounded knobs, hills, and ridges.

Anthropologists and archeologists tell us that some ten thousand years ago, these mountains were populated by an Indian tribe that left complex burial mounds suggestive of elaborate rituals and ceremonies. Why the early Indians abandoned the region, no one knows, but they inspired a rich lore of folktales and legends of demons, spirits, ghosts, and witches, all of which allegedly haunt the range to this day.

In 1835, a man named Francis J. Kron came to the Uwharrie Mountains. From somewhere in Europe, Kron had arrived on the east coast several years earlier, had repeatedly run into trouble with the law, and had finally moved westward. He eventually came to the Uwharrie Mountains, traveling alone and on foot. For months, Kron lived deep in the woods, appearing on rare occasions at small area settlements to purchase supplies.

Kron was a dark-complected, sharp-featured, angular man with shoulder-length black hair. Though he claimed to be a doctor, it is doubtful he ever received a medical education from any established institution. A few of the local residents, though, let Kron doctor their ailments. They reported his methods of treatment were bizarre, using wild herbs and strange powders, and sing-song chanting in a language no one understood. Many of the area residents began to believe that Kron was evil and that he was somehow linked with the mountain demons, spirits, and curses of the old folktales.

Within a few years, Kron married a local woman, a wealthy widow, and immediately purchased a plantation near what is now the town of Albemarle. Kron built a mansion, bought numerous slaves to work on his farm, and prospered.

A few months after the wedding, Kron's wife disappeared and was never seen again. No explanation was ever offered. Visitors to the Kron mansion were never greeted and often left without seeing a soul on the farm. Stories of bonfires and odd ceremonies on the Kron plantation spread throughout the area.

Around 1879, Kron hired a man named Dan Compton to do odd jobs around the plantation. Compton lived in one of the old slave cabins and took his meals with the hired help. Once, Kron ordered Compton into a dark room deep in the mansion and showed him a large keg standing in the center of the room. The top of the keg was nailed shut and heavy steel bands were secured tightly around the oak staves. Kron told Compton to roll the keg into the middle of one of the large fields.

The keg was heavy and unwieldy, but Compton managed to wrestle it from the house and roll it to the prescribed site, accompanied by the evil-looking Kron. As he rolled the keg along the ground, Compton noted that it jingled as if it were filled with coins. About halfway to the field, Compton pleaded with Kron to let him to rest. The plantation owner granted the handyman a few moments to catch his breath, and as Compton sat on the tipped-over keg, he noticed a small space between two of the oak staves. He saw that the keg was filled with gold coins. Compton assumed Kron intended to bury the keg of coins.

When the two men arrived at the designated site, Kron told Compton to set the keg upright and pile some boards around it. Nearby were three torn-down slave shacks, and from them Compton took dozens of pieces of milled lumber, stacking them around the keg as ordered. When Compton finished, Kron ordered the handyman to leave and never return to the site.

That evening, Compton was awakened by the sound of loud chanting. From the doorway of his cabin, he could see a huge bonfire out in the large field where he had rolled the keg of gold coins. He could just make out human figures leaping and swaying to some primitive rhythm.

Slipping on pants and shoes, Compton crept closer to the fire, keeping to the trees at the edge of the field. When he stopped some fifty yards from the blaze where he could observe the goings-on, he saw Kron and several Indians he had never seen before dancing naked around the huge fire and chanting in a language he had never heard.

In the middle of the blaze, the wooden staves of the keg were burning away and the gold coins were beginning to melt. Ochre streams of molten metal flowed lazily from the pyre, and then cooled into shapeless masses. As the gold melted, the screams and chants of the dancers grew louder and more passionate. Frightened and appalled, Compton fled from the scene. Reaching his cabin, he snatched up his few possessions and left the Uwharries, never to return.

Years later on his deathbed, Compton related for the first time the story of that strange autumn night of 1878. Asked why he had never told it before, he said he was afraid of Kron, afraid that he was some kind of demon and had the power to call down a terrible curse on him. Magic and witchcraft were a powerful part of the beliefs of many people in those days, and Compton, who was susceptible to such notions, never returned to the plantation for any of the gold he was certain still lay in the field.

The old Kron place was just northwest of present-day Morrow Mountain State Park. The field on which Kron held the strange rituals lies between a small unnamed creek and the Louder Ferry Road. Immediately south of the field is Hattaway Mountain. Somewhere near the center of that field, beneath a few inches of soil, likely lies a shapeless mass of gold worth millions of dollars.

Outlaw Treasure Cave Near Hendersonville

For years caves have been favored haunts of outlaws. Caves were normally far removed from settlements and thus afforded isolation; caves offered simple yet effective protection from the elements—they were cool in the summer and warm in the winter; and caves were ideal places to hide loot.

One such cave exists in Henderson County. History reveals that this cave often served as a temporary home for renegades and as a repository for stolen gold, silver, and currency. History has not, however, revealed whether any of the hidden treasure has been recovered from this cave.

The story of the Henderson County treasure cave came to light with the discovery of the diary of Lieutenant J.W. Hadley, a Union officer. Hadley's company fought Confederate forces during the famous Battle of the Wilderness in 1864 in eastern Virginia. Early in the fighting, Hadley was wounded and captured and, along with hundreds of other Union prisoners, shipped by rail to Columbia, South Carolina, where he was interned in a prison camp.

The prison camp was a makeshift assemblage of poorly constructed shacks in a disease-ridden swamp. Each day, men died from dysentery and malaria. Hadley and three companions plotted to escape the dreadful confinement.

One night, the four men fled the prison, and once out of range of pursuit, undertook the long journey northward, hoping to encounter Union forces. For days the men slunk through the woods, keeping to low areas and dense brush to avoid being seen. Sometimes they hid from roving patrols of Rebel soldiers.

Where they could get them, the men fed on wild berries and small game. The difficult travel, the hunger and the hiding, slowed the fugitives' journey, and an unusually cold autumn overtook them as they crossed the border into North Carolina.

With the frigid temperatures, wild berries were scarce, and the men resorted to stealing frost-killed vegetables from gardens on the outskirts of small communities. In one raid on a garden patch, the four men were surprised by the arrival of three women who had come to harvest greens. The women were armed, and while the fugitives were held at gunpoint, the youngest ran back up the trail in search of help.

Presently, a tall bearded old man returned with the young woman. He was carrying a rifle and had a vengeful gleam in his eye. He noted the ragged and torn Union blue uniforms on the haggard men and told them he had no use for Yankees or thieves. Hadley and his companions dropped to their knees and pleaded for their lives, swearing they intended no harm and only wanted to get food and leave the region as soon as possible.

The old man took pity on the starved, ragged soldiers. Though he was a bred-in-the-bone Southerner who believed in the Confederate cause and had lost two sons to Union bullets, the man lowered his rifle and invited the fugitives to his cabin, where he saw to it they were fed a proper meal.

During dinner, the host suggested to Hadley it might be prudent to hire a guide to lead them to Union sanctuary. He said he knew a man who might deliver them to Knoxville for a hundred dollars in gold coins. Hadley agreed, the man was sent for, and he arrived at the cabin late the next day. The newcomer was a quiet, thin, dark man whose black bowler hat shadowed his face. After listening to the fugitives' tale of escape and flight, he agreed to let Hadley pay him the hundred dollars on arrival at Knoxville since none of the escapees had any money. He told the four he would return with horses after sundown the next evening.

The following night, a quiet knock at the cabin door preceded a deep voice announcing that all was ready and they must depart at once. When Hadley and his companions assembled outside the cabin, the guide told them they would be blindfolded and that they would soon understand the reason for the precaution. Each was helped onto a horse, and they were led into the woods. As they rode along, Hadley made mental notes of the journey. He recalled later that while he didn't know which way they went on leaving the cabin, they were on horseback for about an hour, and he recalled that they crossed two shallow creeks near the end of the ride. Eventually the guide called a halt, and the four blindfolded men were helped off their horses. After a brief hike up a moderately steep gravel slope, they were led to a guide-rope. Following the rope, the men came into what was unmistakably a large cave. After several more minutes of walking, they were ordered to halt and their blindfolds were removed.

Hadley saw they were in a large torch-lit chamber. He could hear water dripping some distance away and occasionally heard voices coming from some far passageway. Against one wall of the cave were piled several saddlebags and chests.

The guide handed each man a blanket and told them to sleep, as they would depart early in the morning. They would have this chamber to themselves, he said, but they were not to leave it. He told them a guard was stationed in the passageway with orders to shoot anyone who tried to escape.

During the night, Hadley found it difficult to sleep. He threw off his blanket, removed one of the burning torches from a niche in the cave wall, and explored the chamber. When he arrived at the pile of saddlebags and chests in the far corner, he regarded them with interest. Hadley noted the chests were of the type railroad companies used to transport gold, silver, and currency. Bending to one of the saddlebags, he unfastened the straps and peered within. His heart pounded as he saw what must have been hundreds of gold coins. He opened several more of the packs and found gold or silver coins in each. He guessed the chests held a fortune in gold and silver as well. Hadley began to understand the reason for the blindfolds—he and his companions were being held in a cave used by bandits to store treasure! Hadley returned to his blanket but could not sleep.

Early the next morning, six rough-looking men entered the chamber. Each was carrying a heavy saddlebag which was added to the pile against the far wall. Pretending sleep, Hadley listened to the conversations of the newcomers and learned that they were robbers and smugglers and that the cave was a indeed a repository for their booty.

A few minutes later, the guide came and told the four fugitives it was time to leave. The six newly-arrived men would go with them to Knoxville, he said, since they were all headed that way anyway.

Hadley and his companions were once again blindfolded and led from the cave. Outside, they were ordered to rest near a grove of trees while their hosts sealed the entrance. As he waited, Hadley managed to adjust his blindfold so he could see what the workers were doing. The bandits piled boulders in front of the low cave entrance, covering it and making it look much like the rest of the talus-covered slope. When this was done, the outlaws gathered in front of the camouflaged entrance and swore an oath of secrecy about the location of the treasure cave.

Presently all were mounted and riding north. After about a mile, the guide told the soldiers they could remove their blindfolds. After doing so, Hadley glanced about for prominent landmarks, but all he could see was the dense grove of beech trees where they had stopped and a small creek across which was a thick oak forest. The rest of the journey was uneventful, and a few days later, they reached the outskirts of Knoxville and a Union Army camp.

The bandits held one of the fugitives hostage and told Hadley and the two others to go into the camp and get the promised hundred dollars. Hadley and his companions were escorted to the tent of a company commander, where they told the incredible story of their capture, escape, and flight through the Southern countryside. After some initial disbelief, the officer accepted Hadley's tale and told his aide to bring him a hundred dollars. There was no gold in the camp, and the aide came back with paper currency. The commander told Hadley to offer the bandits the currency and sent him off in the company of two armed soldiers.

The bandits were understandably nervous when Hadley returned in the company of the armed escort, but when they saw the fee was in paper money instead of gold they were furious. Hadley explained there was no gold in the camp and pleaded for the outlaws to take the money. The discussion grew heated, and one of the bandits pulled a gun and fired at a trooper, killing him instantly. While Hadley and the hostage ducked for cover, the outlaws fired at the second trooper, who took shelter behind a tree. Frustrated, the outlaws reined their horses around and dashed back to the south.

Hearing the commotion, the company commander assembled two dozen troops and set out in pursuit of the outlaws. About five miles from the hostage exchange site, the soldiers overtook the fleeing desperadoes and a gunfight ensued. After a half hour of exchanging gunfire, all of the outlaws and three of the Union troopers lay dead. When the outcome was reported to Hadley later in the day, he realized that all the men who knew where the treasure cave was had died with the secret.

When the war ended, Hadley returned to Henderson County to seek the treasure cave. With some difficulty, he found the small farm where he and his companions were first discovered. He looked up the old farmer who had fed them and arranged their escape, and thanked him for saving their lives.

Hadley was sure the treasure cave was still sealed and the gold and silver coins lay untouched deep within the large chamber where he had first sen them. He set up a small camp near the cabin and spent the next several weeks walking and riding through the forest in search of the cave. With no visual landmarks to guide him, Hadley had trouble retracing the route he had followed blindfolded two years earlier. After successive failures, he finally gave up and went home.

Hadley returned to Henderson County many times over the next twenty years, but each trip was no more successful than the one before it, and he never found the elusive cave. On his deathbed, Hadley said he was certain the cave had never been reopened and the treasure was still intact.

Others have tried to follow Hadley's directions to the hoard, but to date none of it has been recovered.

Lost Keg of Gold

Deep in a forgotten gold mine in the Union County region of the South Carolina Appalachians rests an old nail keg half-filled with gold mined from a rich vein. The keg of gold, along with its owner, were buried in an 1858 cave-in, and all attempts to retrieve the fortune have failed.

Two years before the Civil War, life in the Piedmont region of South Carolina was slow and uneventful. An easy peace lay across the mountains, the valley, and the area farms. As it would for years to come, cotton reigned. Large landowners with plenty of slaves were wealthy and powerful.

Asa Smyth was one such landowner. He had three thousand acres of rich farmland that, with the help of his hundred slaves, produced healthy crops of cotton each year. Smyth was hard on his slaves, just as likely to whip them as to look at them. One of the slaves, a tall, strong, older man Smyth called Blue, was a particular favorite because he was a natural leader and just as hard a taskmaster as his owner. Smyth elevated Blue to foreman and charged him with the daily operation of the cotton farm.

In the winter, when the fields lay fallow, Smyth worked his slaves in the nearby Hopkins Mine. The mine had operated for several years and been productive, but poor management had caused it to close down. Smyth took out a lease on the mine, and when his cotton was in, he put his slaves to work digging gold.

Smyth and Blue would wake the slaves before dawn and, following behind in a horse-drawn wagon, run them the two miles to the mine where they would work until sundown. Many slaves died in the mine, but neither the owner nor the foreman showed any mercy.

Each morning as Blue was readying the slaves, Smyth loaded an old nail keg into the wagon. Gold dug from the mine went in the keg. Soon it was too heavy for Smyth to lift into the wagon by himself, and Blue was enlisted to help. As more gold was added to the keg, it got so heavy that Smyth began keeping it at the mine. Deep in the gold mine and alongside one of the main shafts, Smyth had his slaves dig a chamber which he referred to as his "room." The low-ceilinged little room was sparsely furnished with a wooden table and chair. Here Smyth would sort and weigh his gold before adding it to the store in the keg.

Smyth oversaw the work done by the slaves, recommending the excavation of new shafts and supervising the cleaning and processing of the gold. At the end of each day, Smyth would have Blue line up the slaves and check their hair to make certain no gold was caught—or cached—in it. This done, the slaves were marched back to the plantation.

March of 1859 was wetter than normal. It rained hard every day. Parts of the Hopkins Mine flooded and Smyth put several slaves to hand-pumping the knee-deep water out of several shafts. To compound the problems, one of the main shafts suffered a minor cave-in.

As March wore on, Smyth was still adding gold to his growing fortune—the keg was now a little more than half full. While sorting the gold one afternoon in his room, Smyth called for his foreman, who came running. Smyth, standing ankle deep in water, told Blue he was feeling chilled and sent him to the wagon for his coat. When the foreman reached the wagon, parked about a hundred feet from the mine entrance, he heard a loud rumble and felt the earth shake. He turned back toward the entrance and saw a great cloud of dust roll from the shaft and disperse into the clear outside air.

Blue ran to the entrance, calling through the thick dust hanging in the shaft. Several slaves came stumbling and crawling out of the shaft and told him a cave-in had destroyed a large section of the mine, killed many of the workers, and completely buried the chamber where Smyth was counting his gold.

Blue leaped into the wagon and drove rapidly to the plantation, where he told Smyth's wife, Sara, of the accident. She told the foreman to get some of the neighbors and try to reach the chamber to see if Asa could be rescued.

Within hours, about two dozen people had gathered at the entrance of the old Hopkins mine. An exploratory party of several men entered the shaft but came out after only a few minutes, telling the gathering crowd that the cave-in had destroyed most of the mine and no one could have possibly survived.

Over the years, several attempts were made to excavate the collapsed rock and debris from the old Hopkins Mine to retrieve Asa Smyth's keg of gold. While tons of material have been removed from the first hundred feet of the original shaft, most of the passageways remain filled. Asa Smyth's chamber, according to Blue, was about a thousand feet deep in the mine, and the room that held the keg of gold and Asa Smyth's bones was blocked by tons of debris.

An excavation company tried to reopen the mine in the early 1930s but was defeated by the tons of rock it would have to remove. The workers were also constantly threatened with new cave-ins.

Somewhere deep in the old Hopkins Mine in a room carved out of mountain rock, like a mausoleum, a nail keg half-filled with gold lies next to the bones of Asa Smyth.

The Indian Gold Mine de Soto Never Found

One of the most fascinating and enduring lost mine legends in South Carolina tells of a rich lode of gold known to the local Indians and at one time sought by the famed Spanish explorer Hernando de Soto. The mine, probably in present-day Pickens County, was never found by the intrepid de Soto, and for centuries it was apparently a primary source of the gold used by several area Indian tribes to make fine jewelry, ornaments, and icons.

As de Soto traveled and explored the southern Appalachians, he thought always of his mission to locate, excavate, and ship back to Spain any and all kinds of precious metals. When he stumbled across a gold or silver mine operated by Indians, he would often enslave the members of the tribe and force them to dig the ore for Spain. If the Indians resisted, de Soto would kill several of the tribe's leaders as an example. Thus, the gold-hungry Spaniard subjugated, tortured, and killed hundreds of Indians in his quest for wealth for the Spanish king.

At an Indian village called Nepetaca in what is now southern Georgia, a young Indian who was about to be tortured by de Soto's men pleaded for mercy, telling his captors he knew of a wealthy gold mine in the mountains several marches to the north. The mine was supposed to be a three-day ride from a large Indian village called Cofitachiqui, which was ruled by a queen.

The soldiers brought the young man to de Soto, and the explorer listened with interest to the story. He decided to go to Cofitachiqui, and ordered his men to get ready to leave immediately. De Soto had one of his priests baptize the young Indian, gave him the Christian name of Peter, and incorporated him into his army.

The Spanish force left Nepetaca in March, 1540, and for several weeks traveled north through the plains, forests, and swamps of the humid lowlands. Provisions were running dangerously low, hunting was poor, and the progress and morale of the party was deteriorating rapidly. Whenever the Spaniards sighted an Indian village, they would prepare to raid it for food and women only to find each time it was infested with smallpox brought to the region by an earlier Spanish explorer, Vasquez de Ayllon. De Soto's army gave each such village a wide berth.

Several times, de Soto was ready to abandon the quest for the mine, but young Peter always reassured him that the waiting riches would make the toil and sacrifices worthwhile.

But after weeks of weary marching and being forced to eat dogs and horses, an angry and frustrated de Soto ordered the young Indian killed. Juan Ortiz, de Soto's chief interpreter, argued for Peter's life, saying that the boy's knowledge of the local language would prove useful and could mean the difference between life and death. De Soto relented, and four days later, the young Indian led the party of Spaniards to the outskirts of Cofitachiqui.

The village lay spread along the flood plain of the Savannah River about a dozen miles downstream from present-day Augusta, Georgia, on the South Carolina side of the River. The village housed large families in its many circular earthen structures, and had been spared the smallpox epidemic that had decimated tribes farther south. The inhabitants of Cofitachiqui were friendly, cultured, and courteous.

As de Soto and his men rode into the village, they were warmly greeted by the Indians and invited to a welcoming feast. The Spaniards were brought gifts of fresh-water pearls, fine furs, and food.

Looking around at the Indian population, de Soto noticed much gold. Many of the Indians were wearing armbands, rings, and ornate headpieces made from it.

During the feast, the queen of the village came to the Spanish leader. De Soto wrote in his journals that the queen was tall, almost statuesque, light of color, and very attractive. De Soto called the queen *la Señora,* and he thanked her when she personally welcomed the Spaniards and invited them to set up camp near the village.

Playing the role of the grateful guest, de Soto agreed to remain for a few days, but uppermost in his mind was gold. A casual walk through the Indian village revealed that the dwellings and temples were filled with gold icons and ornaments. De Soto even saw ceremonial ax blades and spearheads made from the precious metal.

He asked for and was granted an audience with *la Señora,* and during their conversation, he asked where the wealth he saw in the village had come from. The queen would not be specific, but did tell the Spaniard that for many generations the Indians had excavated gold from a mine in the mountains to the north. She claimed the mine had an unending supply of the precious ore and would provide the metal for her people for centuries to come.

That evening, greed overtaking gratitude, de Soto made plans to kidnap *la Señora* and force her to guide him to the mine.

At dawn the following day, the Spanish soldiers swarmed into the village, sacked the temples, and seized the queen and several of her followers. De Soto told *la Señora* that she was to guide him and his army to the rich gold mine in the north or they would all be tortured and killed. The queen and her followers agreed to show the Spaniard the mine, and the party began to wind its way through the low foothills of western South Carolina toward the higher reaches of the mountains looming miles ahead of them.

Progress was slowed dramatically when spring rains struck the second day of the journey. Torrents fell for days on the Spanish army and its captives, making travel nearly impossible at times. Flood waters washed out trails, and the company got lost more than once. Rivers were often too high and swift to ford, forcing the travelers to wait days to cross. The horses were slowed by the soft muck of the trails.

Word had spread to Indian villages north of Cofitachiqui that the queen had been taken by the Spaniards, and each time the army approached a village, they were met with hostility and sometimes attacked. Several soldiers were killed, food again became scarce, and de Soto's confidence began to suffer.

The journey that was to take only days dragged into weeks. The Spaniards were weary and frustrated, and de Soto was beginning to worry about dissension. The soldiers were tired of difficult marching and going days without food. The men guarding the queen and her subordinates grew more careless each day, and one evening, *la Señora* and her followers saw their chance and escaped.

De Soto, having lost his hostage and guide to the rich gold mine, became discouraged and surly. Fearing he would soon lose control of his army, he ordered them to abandon the quest. Turning their backs on the Appalachian Mountains, the party of explorers marched west toward the lowlands, reaching the Mississippi River many weeks later.

Scholars, prospectors, geologists, and students of this tale of a lost gold mine in the South Carolina Appalachians have often debated whether the lode really exists, but some facts support that it does. First, there *was* an abundance of gold in the village of Cofitachiqui. Second, the Indians had little reason for lying about the source of the ore, for to them it was used merely for ornaments and ceremony and had no value as a medium of exchange. Third, gold has been found elsewhere in the South Carolina Appalachians. There are impressive deposits in both Pickens and York Counties.

De Soto was probably only a day or two from the famed Indian gold mine of the Appalachians, but the hardship of his journey, coupled with the escape of his prisoners, caused him to abandon the quest.

The incident was the first of the difficulties and bad luck that would plague the Spanish leader. While his party did cross the wide Mississippi River and find gold in the Ozark and Ouachita Mountains to the west, de Soto's health was starting to deteriorate. Many of his soldiers deserted, several with fortunes in gold and silver gained in the expedition. Eventually de Soto became delirious and had to be carried on a litter. The Spaniard, an important early explorer of the southern United States, died somewhere near the Arkansas–Louisiana border while trying to get back to Spain.

The lost mine of the South Carolina Appalachians was said to be a rich source of almost pure gold for the local Indians, who were probably members of the Creek tribe. When the area was abandoned during the infamous Trail of Tears resettlement, the mine was closed and probably covered over. Many have searched for it over the past century and a half, yet it remains lost.

Silver Mine in Pickens County

Gold lured de Soto to explore western and north-western South Carolina, and according to the tales and legends passed down over the centuries, gold was indeed plentiful. Silver, however, was equally abundant, and like the fabled gold, eludes modern-day treasure hunters.

One legend of lost silver from this region tells of a small exploration party of Spaniards, most likely a detachment from de Soto's army under the leadership of Juan de Villalobos, that dug ore from a hillside by an Indian village near the present-day junction of Anderson, Oconee, and Pickens counties.

The Spaniards asked permission from the Indians to mine the silver. It was freely granted. During the following few weeks, the Spaniards bartered their possessions to the Indians for food. The vein of silver the Spaniards followed into the rock was so rich that excavating it left them no time to hunt for food. Soon, though, the newcomers ran out of items to trade to the Indians.

The leader of the Spanish mining expedition ordered the Indians to hunt and fish for his men, but they refused. Enraged, de Villalobos enslaved them, tortured and killed many, forced the rest to work in the mine, and stole their stores of food.

During the roundup of slaves, several Indians escaped into the woods and fled to a neighboring village. There the refugees told what had happened, and the Indians plotted to attack the Spaniards, free their brothers, and drive the intruders from the country.

Weeks went by, and the Spaniards grew complacent. Never threatened, they saw little need to post guards.

One night, by the light of a full moon, a large force of Indians crept through the woods to the Spaniards' bivouac and slew them all in their blankets. They carried the bodies deep into the mine shaft and covered the entrance. The Indians thereafter regarded the site as evil and cursed, and they moved their village far away. The story of the rich silver mine was told and retold over successive generations, becoming part of the tribal folklore, but the location of the mine eventually faded from the memory of the Indians and remains a mystery.

In 1670, an expedition led by a Dr. Henry Woodward arrived at the village of Cofitachiqui on the Savannah River. Woodward, a wealthy British physician, explorer, and ambassador to the New World, befriended the Indians he found in the large settlement and earned their trust. So completely was he incorporated into the tribe that he was given lodging, food, and a prominent place on the village council.

Woodward was familiar with the story of de Soto's visit to Cofitachiqui more than a hundred years earlier and the ill-fated search for the gold mine. Woodward asked several of the Cofitachiqui residents about the tale and was assured every word of it was true, and that, in fact, gold was still being taken in great quantities from the mine.

While living in Cofitachiqui, Woodward also noted an abundance of silver jewelry, icons, and ornaments. When he asked about the source of this ore, he was told that it came from a mine very near the legendary gold mine.

During his stay, Woodward learned approximately where the Indians' gold and silver mines lay, but as he was preparing an expedition to the area, he took sick and died within days. Many believe that the Indians, learning of

Woodward's plans to search for their mines, poisoned his food.

In 1760, during the French and Indian War, a company of British soldiers was returning from a skirmish with hostile Cherokee when they camped on the banks of Little Wilson's Creek adjacent to the Keowee Trail. While encamped, several soldiers noticed some intriguing color in the local rock formations and dug out chunks as souvenirs.

The war kept the soldiers occupied for months thereafter, and when the conflict wound down, the company disbanded and its members dispersed. Later, several men who had dug pieces of the brightly colored rock from the stone matrix near Little Wilson Creek discovered that it was almost pure silver! The former soldiers organized successive attempts to find the original site of their discovery, but always failed. The silver is believed to have been found near Pointing Rock, which is just south of Old Stone Church near Little Wilsons Creek in the western corner of Pickens County.

Around 1815, a Cherokee family was known to have mined pure silver near the settlement of Shainrock, now a ghost town not far from present-day Clemson. The Indians would sometimes sell the silver to travelers and passers-by, but during the 1820s they disappeared. They may have been killed for their presumed wealth and their bodies hidden in a mine, but the truth was never known. Years later, visitors to Shainrock reported finding nuggets of raw silver as well as small clots of the smelted ore. No one has found the source of the Cherokee family's silver, though many have searched.

During the late 1850s, two separate mining companies sank shafts in the area, seeking a vein of silver they suspected was just below the surface. Both reported failure.

Just a year after the two companies withdrew from the region, a small contingent of miners from Charleston arrived, established a well-provisioned camp, located some silver, and successfully mined it for two years.

Operations ceased when the War Between The States broke out. It is not known what became of the miners, but after the war, the abandoned shafts were not reopened, and no one ever came forward to renew the claim.

VIRGINIA & WEST VIRGINIA

VIRGINIA

1. The Mysterious Beale Treasure
2. John Crismo's Buried Coins
3. The Lost Smith Family Treasure
4. The Grey Ghost's Lost Treasure
5. The Snow Hill Farm Treasure

WEST VIRGINIA

6. The Doll House Treasure of Upshur County
7. The Peddler's Lost Cache
8. Hidden Treasure in the Buchannon River Valley

9, 10, 11. Other Tales of Lost and Buried Treasures in West Virginia

The Mysterious Beale Treasure

The best known and most sought-after lost treasure in the state of Virginia is the mysterious and elusive Beale cache. This buried fortune is said to consist of nearly 3,000 pounds of gold, 5,088 pounds of silver, and $13,000 worth of jewels. The Beale treasure has been the subject of books, magazine articles, and television programs, and one network news broadcast said the search for the Beale treasure was one of the longest and costliest in the history of the United States.

Specific directions to the fabulous Beale treasure can be found in three separate codes devised by Beale himself, as far as is known. Only one has ever been deciphered. The other two complex codes, though having been examined by cryptoanalysts and studied by computer and decoding experts, remain unbroken, and the location of the great treasure is as much a mystery today as it was when Thomas Jefferson Beale and eight friends buried it in Bedford County in 1819 and 1821.

Little is known of Beale's life. What is known is that early in 1817, he and twenty-nine other Virginians journeyed westward to New Mexico and Colorado. Two conflicting stories, neither proven, give Beale's reasons for leaving Virginia. One tale is that he shot his neighbor in Fincastle, Virginia, in a fight over a woman. Believing the man dead and fearing he would be hung for the deed, Beale fled west. The second tale, considerably less colorful, is that Beale gathered up friends for a buffalo-hunting and fur-trapping expedition to the western plains and mountains.

Whatever the reason, Beale and his companions eventually found themselves in south-central Colorado, searching for a pass into the higher reaches of the Rocky Mountains, where they planned to hunt beaver. As the party climbed the foothills of the great range, one of the men discovered a thick vein of gold in some exposed rock. Deciding that mining the ore would profit them more than trapping and selling furs, the men spent the next few years systematically excavating the precious metal from the rock matrix of the mountainside. They found silver nearby, and mined great quantities of it, too.

After eighteen months, they had an impressive stockpile of gold and silver. The men, all good friends, agreed to split the fortune evenly. They held a meeting and decided to send Beale and eight others back to Virginia to bury the rich hoard in a safe place. The others would keep working in the mines while awaiting the return of the Beale party.

On a bitterly cold afternoon in late November, Beale and his companions, along with two wagon loads of gold and silver nuggets, arrived at Goose Creek in Bedford County, Virginia. The party followed a narrow and seldom-used trail which paralleled the creek and led into a gap in the foothills of the Blue Ridge Mountains near Peak of the Otters. Once in the pass, Beale looked around until he found what he wanted—a place where he could bury the treasure. Snow began to fall, and the men worked swiftly, digging a square pit six feet deep. As the wind swirled the snow around them, the miners lined the floor and walls of this man-made vault with flat stones they found nearby. Into this chamber they placed the gold and silver from nearly two years' work in the Colorado mines. The nuggets were packed into iron cooking pots, the covers tightly secured with wire. The men filled the hole to the top with dirt and covered it with rocks and forest debris.

Beale and his party rested several days after the long journey from the west. They bought supplies and fresh riding stock, and started back in early December. They rejoined the other miners in the Colorado foothills nearly a month later.

Mining continued, and after almost two more years, another load of gold and silver was ready to be shipped east and buried with the previous cache. Beale was again chosen for the trip. The partners agreed to keep mining until they had enough gold and silver for a third and final trip to Virginia, where they would unearth the rich cache, divide it, and return to a normal life as wealthy men.

One morning in the third week of November in 1821, the wagons were loaded to capacity with the ore. Bidding farewell to those who remained to work in the mines, Beale and his companions began the second long journey back to the Blue Ridge Mountains.

Reaching the cache a little over a month later, Beale and his companions added the second load of gold and silver. When the hole refilled and camouflaged, Beale and his fellows decided to write a description of the secret location and its contents and leave it in the area for the others to find, should something happen to them. Over the next several days, Beale and a few of his partners devised a series of incredibly complex codes. They produced three sheets of paper, each covered with a series of numerals. These three papers have since been called the Beale Code, and have mystified researchers for well over a century.

Cipher Number One allegedly tells how to find the fabulous treasure and remains unbroken to this day. Cipher Number Two describes the complete contents of the treasure vault. Cipher Number Three supposedly lists the names of the thirty men who were to divide the treasure equally.

When the ciphers were completed, they were placed in a metal strongbox fastened with a stout lock. By agreement of the nine men who buried the ore, the locked box was given to one Robert Morris, a man they all knew and trusted. Morris, a quiet gentleman who ran a respectable inn at Lynchburg and often kept valuables for travelers, readily agreed to keep the strongbox for Beale and his friends.

At Morris's invitation, the miners stayed several days at the inn, resting. The day they left for Colorado, Beale told Morris that if someone did not return within ten years to claim the strongbox and its contents, he, Morris, was to open it. Beale also told Morris that within a few weeks he would mail him the information he would need to interpret the codes in the strongbox. Beale and his eight companions rode away from the inn a short time later, disappearing into the dense forest to the west. Morris never saw any of them again.

About two months later, Morris received a short letter from Beale that had been mailed from St. Louis. The letter reiterated what Beale had already told Morris—that the contents of the strongbox would be meaningless without the decoding keys. He said the necessary keys were in a sealed envelope with Morris's address on it. The envelope, according to Beale, was given to a friend in St. Louis with instructions to mail it to Morris in June, 1832. Morris never again heard from Beale, nor did he receive the envelope ten years later.

Although the designated time had elapsed, the trustworthy Morris refused to open the strongbox, thinking that someone from the Beale party would eventually return to claim it. Years passed and Morris soon forgot about the strongbox, which he had hidden away under some clutter in an old shed adjacent to the inn. One day, about twenty-three years after Beale had left the strongbox, Morris chanced upon it while searching the shed for a harness.

When Morris broke open the box, he first saw lying atop the contents a letter addresed to him. In elaborate detail, the letter told of the expedition to the west, the discovery of the gold and silver, and the subsequent trips to the Blue Ridge Mountains to bury the treasure. The letter ended by asking Morris to use the code to find and dig up the treasure. Morris was to divide it into thirty-one equal parts—one for each of the original participants and one for Morris himself.

Morris examined the three pieces of paper which bore the Beale Code. Each was written over with an apparently random series of numbers, ranging from single to quadruple digits. Intrigued, the innkeeper spent many hours trying to decipher the curious arrangements of numbers, but couldn't make any sense of them. For the next several years, Morris tried to decipher the complex Beale Code, but he eventually gave up.

Some time later, when Morris was convinced no one would return to claim the strongbox and its contents, he showed the codes and letters to a friend, James Ward. For months Ward pored over the three pieces of paper and eventually broke Cipher Number Two.

Purely by accident, Ward discovered this code was based on the Declaration of Independence. When finally deciphered, it read:

> I have deposited in the county of Bedford about four miles from Buford's Inn in an excavation or vault six feet below the surface of the ground the following articles belonging to the parties whose names are given in number three herewith. The first deposit was ten hundred and fourteen pounds of gold and thirty-eight hundred pounds of silver. This was deposited November, 1819. The second deposit was made December, 1821, and consisted of nineteen hundred and seven pounds of gold and twelve hundred and eighty-eight pounds of silver. Also jewels obtained in St. Louis in exchange to save transportation and valued at thirteen thousand dollars. The above is packed securely in iron pots with iron covers. The vault is lined with

> stones and the vessels lie on solid rock and are covered with other stones. Paper number one describes the exact location of the vault so no difficulty will be had in finding it.

Ward, suspecting the other two codes would likewise be deciphered by using the Declaration of Independence, eagerly tackled them, but was soon disappointed to learn that they apparently had separate and independent keys. Ward was particularly interested in breaking Cipher Number One, which allegedly gave directions to the treasure site, but could make no sense of it whatsoever. *(The code, containing 520 numbers, is reproduced in its entirety at the end of the story.)*

Ward worked on the two unbroken codes for several months before giving up. With Morris's permission, Ward made the codes public.

Ever since the Beale Code was made known, hundreds of people—cryptographers, computer programmers, historians, treasure hunters, adventurers—have tried to decipher it. For many years, the Blue Ridge Mountains in and around Bedford County were fairly teeming with those who thought they had an inside track on the treasure. To date, however, the first and third codes remain unbroken, and the fabulous treasure is still hidden.

Although the Beale treasure is Virginia's best-known and most sought, many believe it is nothing more than an elaborate hoax and that Thomas Jefferson Beale never existed! Skeptics have suggested that innkeeper Morris and his friend Ward fabricated the entire story. They point out that Thomas Jefferson, the third president of the United States and author of the Declaration of Independence, on which one code was based, had a penchant for writing in numerical codes and ciphers. It may also be worth noting that a man named Beale brought word to the east of the fantastic gold finds in California during the early 1800s.

If the Beale treasure is a hoax, two things remain to be explained. First of all, what would have been the purpose of such a trick? There appears no obvious or profitable motive for such a sophisticated and elaborate hoax. Both Morris and Ward shunned any kind of publicity, and neither profited from his association with the Beale treasure. Secondly, the sheer intricacy of the codes makes it seem unlikely to have been devised merely as a prank.

The Beale treasure probably does, in fact, exist and in exactly the amounts indicated by Beale himself in Cipher Two. Many who have researched the Beale story over the years have agreed on the authenticity of the events, the treasure, and the codes.

Beale Cipher Number One:

71, 194, 38, 1701, 89, 76, 11, 83, 1629, 48, 94, 63, 132, 16, 111, 95, 84, 341, 975, 14, 40, 64, 27, 81, 139, 213, 63, 90, 1120, 8, 15, 3, 126, 2018, 40, 74, 758, 485, 604, 230, 436, 664, 582, 150, 251, 284, 308, 231, 124, 211, 486, 225, 401, 370, 11, 101, 305, 139, 189, 17, 33, 88, 208, 193, 145, 1, 94, 73, 416, 918, 263, 28, 500, 538, 356, 117, 136, 219, 27, 176, 130, 10, 460, 25, 485, 18, 436, 65, 84, 200, 283, 118, 320, 138, 36, 416, 280, 15, 71, 224, 961, 44, 16, 401, 39, 88, 61, 304, 12, 21, 24, 283, 134, 92, 63, 246, 486, 682, 7, 219, 184, 360, 780, 18, 64, 463, 474, 131, 160, 79, 73, 440, 95, 18, 64, 581, 34, 69, 128, 367, 461, 17, 81, 12, 103, 820, 62, 116, 97, 103, 862, 70, 60, 1317, 471, 540, 208, 121, 890, 346, 36, 150, 59, 568, 614, 13, 120, 63, 219, 812, 2160, 1780, 99, 35, 18, 21, 136, 872, 15, 28, 170, 88, 4, 30, 44, 112, 18, 147, 436, 195, 320, 37, 122, 113, 6, 140, 8, 120, 305, 42, 58, 461, 44, 106, 301, 13, 408, 680, 93, 86, 116, 530, 82, 568, 9, 102, 38, 416, 89, 71, 216, 728, 965, 818, 2, 38, 121, 195, 14, 326, 148, 234, 18, 55, 131, 234, 361, 824, 5, 81, 623, 48, 961, 19, 26, 33, 10, 1101, 365, 92, 88, 181, 275, 346, 201, 206, 86, 36, 219, 320, 829, 840, 68, 326, 19, 48, 122, 65, 216, 284, 919, 861, 326, 985, 233, 64, 68, 232, 431, 960, 50, 29, 81, 216, 321, 603, 14, 612, 81, 360, 36, 51, 62, 194, 78, 60, 200, 314, 676, 112, 4, 28, 18, 61, 136, 247, 819, 921, 1060, 464, 895, 10, 6, 66, 119, 38, 41, 49, 612, 423, 962, 302, 294, 875, 78, 14, 23, 111, 109, 62, 31, 501, 823, 216, 280, 34, 24, 150, 1000, 162, 286, 19, 21, 17, 340, 19, 242, 31, 86, 234, 140, 607, 115, 33, 191, 67, 104, 86, 52, 88, 16, 80, 121, 67, 95, 122, 216, 548, 96, 11, 201, 77, 364, 218, 65, 667, 890, 236, 154, 211, 10, 98, 34, 119, 56, 216, 119, 71, 218, 1164, 1496, 1817, 51, 39, 210, 36, 3, 19, 540, 232, 22, 141, 617, 84, 290, 80, 46, 207, 411, 150, 29, 38, 46, 172, 85, 194, 36, 261, 543, 897, 624, 18, 212, 416, 127, 931, 19, 4, 63, 96, 12, 101, 418, 16, 140, 230, 460, 538, 19, 27, 88, 612, 1431, 90, 716, 275, 74, 83, 11, 426, 89, 72, 84, 1300, 1706, 814, 221, 132, 40, 102, 34, 858, 975, 1101, 84, 16, 79, 23, 16, 81, 122, 324, 403, 912, 227, 936, 447, 55, 86, 34, 43, 212, 107, 96, 314, 264, 1065, 323, 428, 601, 203, 124, 95, 216, 814, 2906, 654, 820, 2, 301, 112, 176, 213, 71, 87, 96, 202, 35, 10, 2, 41, 17, 84, 221, 736, 820, 214, 11, 60, 760.

John Crismo's Buried Coins

Early one autumn morning in 1887 on a remote ranch near Pecos, Texas, a young cowhand was trying to wake his bunkhouse companion, an elderly cowboy named John Crismo. When Crismo did not respond to his call, the boy walked over to his bunk and tried to shake him awake. The old man was dead.

The foreman was summoned, a burial was arranged, and as the owner of the ranch searched Crismo's belongings for the name of a relative, he chanced upon an old and well-worn diary. It held fascinating details of buried treasure, a treasure that may today be worth nearly four million dollars, and yet still lies buried beneath a few inches of soil and rock on a lonely mountainside in western Virginia.

The ranch owner pored over the often unintelligible handwriting in Crismo's diary and over several weeks pieced together the story of the buried fortune.

In 1846, when the United States declared war on Mexico, a very young John Crismo enlisted in the army in his home state of New York. Before leaving for foreign soil, Crismo got engaged to a local girl, and they agreed to marry when his enlistment was over. While Crismo was in Mexico, however, his betrothed fell ill, dying only days before he returned.

He never recovered from the loss of his sweetheart. He visited her grave, then mounted his horse and rode out of New York, never to return. For years, the young man roamed the wilderness of Pennsylvania and Ohio, keeping to himself and living like an Indian deep in the woods, craving neither the sight nor company of other humans.

When the War Between The States erupted, Crismo, wishing to return to combat, rode eastward into Pennsylvania, enlisted in the Union army, and was assigned to a cavalry regiment that was immediately ordered to Virginia.

Crismo's unit made several raids on farms and communities in western Virginia, taking livestock, food, and arms and often filling their own pockets with stolen money. In time, the cavalry force became little more than a gang of bandits robbing and looting its way across the Appalachian landscape.

One day, the unit was sent to patrol an area in southwestern Virginia, in Tazewell County. The men, about twenty-four in number, camped on the side of a mountain that overlooked a long narrow valley, flat and richly productive. At one end of the attractive valley was a mansion, and the prospect of finding something valuable at the fine home appealed to the raiding troops.

The valley and everything in it belonged to the eccentric James Grierson. Grierson, who had inherited a fortune, made another from cotton and livestock. The old bachelor owned thirty slaves and was thought the wealthiest man in western Virginia. He was reputed to be worth nearly a million dollars, a staggering amount at the time.

When the war broke out, Grierson, concerned about the safety of his fortune, withdrew all of his money from the area banks and converted it into gold coins. With the help of his favorite slave, Grierson packed the coins into canvas bags and buried them behind his barn.

Anticipating a successful raid, the cavalrymen rode into the valley and overran Grierson's farm, taking the owner prisoner and hanging him by his wrists from a tree limb in the yard. Throughout an intense and sometimes brutal interrogation, Grierson steadfastly refused to reveal where he'd buried his fortune, and the Union raiders soon realized that the old man preferred death to giving up his wealth. Grierson apparently did not survive his interrogation.

While Grierson was being tortured, Crismo befriended the old slave who knew where the plantation owner's fortune lay. With some cajoling and the promise of freedom, Crismo convinced the slave to show him where Grierson's wealth was buried. The slave took Crismo behind the barn, dug about two feet down, and pulled up one of the heavy sacks of gold coins. Crismo looked at it and told the slave not to tell any of the other cavalrymen about the treasure.

Several days later, the cavalry unit was assigned to another area several miles away. Once they had established camp and were awaiting further orders, Crismo returned to the Grierson farm under cover of night, and with the help of the old slave, dug up all the gold coins buried behind the barn. The two men loaded the gold onto a pair of horses and hauled it to where the cavalry had camped before raiding the Grierson plantation. A short distance from the old campground, Crismo and the black man dug a large hole, deposited the coins, and covered the cache with rocks and forest debris. Then they started for the new cavalry encampment. On the way, Crismo handed the old slave a fistful of gold coins he had taken from one of the sacks, and gave the man his freedom.

Crismo told none of his companions about the Grierson fortune when he returned. That night, by the dim light of the fire, Crismo sketched in his ragged diary a crude map showing about where the gold coins lay. In his rough and clumsy grammar, he added descriptions of the terrain and landmarks. The next day, the cavalry unit left Tazewell County for a new assignment in the eastern part of the state.

As the war went on, the regiment fought in several skirmishes, and in one, Crismo was seriously wounded. After a lengthy recovery in a field hospital, he was granted an honorable discharge and sent on his way. He first thought of returning to Tazewell County and digging up the gold, but continuing military action there would have made that difficult. So Crismo took his few belongings and traveled westward instead, roaming the country and regaining his health while biding his time until he could return to Virginia for the gold.

For many years, Crismo wandered the sparsely settled regions west of the Mississippi River, eventually finding his way to Texas. Traveling from town to town and taking odd jobs, the former Union cavalryman barely earned enough to survive. His few diary entries during this time suggest that the wound Crismo had suffered was giving him some serious problems and causing great pain. His writings also suggest that he was not mentally sound at that time.

Years passed, and Crismo eventually landed a job as a cowhand on a ranch near Pecos, Texas. Though much older than most cowboys and quite infirm, he proved a consistent and loyal worker up to the day he quietly passed away in his sleep.

In the years that followed, Crismo's diary passed through several hands and eventually wound up in the possession of a Pecos County man who decided to seek out the buried cache of coins. Using the clumsily-drawn, faded, and somewhat vague map, the searcher arrived at a small Virginia settlement called Aberdeen. Just north of the hamlet, the man located the long narrow valley that had once been part of the extensive Grierson plantation. The land was now state property, having reverted to government ownership when Grierson passed away leaving no heirs.

Just north of the old Grierson plantation was a prominent mountain, undoubtedly the one on which Crismo and his cavalry unit camped before attacking the farm. After exploring the mountain for several days, the searcher discovered what must have been the old campground. He found two Union army-issue canteens, numerous shell casings, and other items suggesting a temporary cavalry bivouac. While Crismo's directions were clear enough to this point, his diary entries never actually said on which side of the camp he buried the fortune. For weeks, the treasure hunter searched. He finally gave up and went back to Texas.

Crismo's diary was relegated to a high dusty shelf in a storeroom and in time was lost. The disappointed searcher never tried again to find the treasure.

Others have searched for John Crismo's buried coins. So-called experts, using metal detectors and dowsing rods, have combed the mountainside near the old cavalry camp, trying to find the four-million-dollar cache. No one knows what became of the diary, and the treasure remains hidden to this day.

The Lost Smith Family Treasure

In the years before the Civil War, Abraham Smith and his two sons, Eli and Samuel, owned and operated one of the largest and most successful plantations in western Virginia. Not far from the farm, near the Clinch Mountains, was a large salt works in which the Smith family had an interest. The vast works supplied much of the salt for this part of the South and was a primary source for the Southern army as well.

Early on the morning of October 2, 1864, Abraham Smith learned that a large Union cavalry contingent, led by the ruthless General George Stoneman, was rapidly approaching the valley. Smith decided to hide the family fortune lest it be found and seized by the Yankees. He hurriedly gathered up approximately fifty-eight thousand dollars' worth of gold and silver coins and jewelry, and with the help of his sons, buried it in the middle of a partially completed roadbed that led to the salt mines near Saltville.

Stoneman, with orders to destroy the salt works and thus disrupt Confederate army supply and cause economic havoc in the area, led his Union force into the valley late that morning, just after the Smiths finished burying their fortune.

Stoneman expected little resistance in the valley, and was therefore surprised when a large combined force of citizens and Confederate soldiers met him. Southern scouts had warned area residents of the approaching Yankees. The hastily assembled force of farmers, laborers, and Rebel soldiers engaged the Union cavalry in a fierce battle. After nearly an hour of fighting, Stoneman called for a retreat. The untrained but enthusiastic Southerners pursued the famous cavalry leader and his troops back through the Cumberland Pass and clear into Kentucky.

After the skirmish, Eli Smith could not be accounted for. He was not among the dead and wounded lying in the valley, and was thought captured by the Yankees and executed along the trail during the disorganized retreat. Though searchers looked for Eli's body for several days, it was never found.

A few days after the battle, Abraham and Samuel Smith returned to the roadbed only to find that the cached jewels and coins had already been dug up and removed, presumably by Union soldiers.

The shock of losing his son and his entire fortune all within the space of a few days was too much for the elderly Abraham Smith, and his health and will to live deteriorated rapidly. Within a year and a half of the battle at the salt works, the old farmer passed away, a broken man.

A few years later, his son Samuel received a strange letter. It was addressed to the late father, but was dated nearly two years earlier, and was from a Corporal Allen E. Brooks, formerly of Stoneman's cavalry unit. Its message surprised and shocked Samuel—it told what had happened to his brother Eli and the buried cache of Smith treasure.

The letter read:

> Kind Sir: I am in pain and upon my deathbed, but I feel I must divest my conscience of a burden that has kept constant company with my soul since shortly after we fought over the salt works there. Your son, Eli, fearing he would be hanged, made a deal with my first sergeant, Jack Harrington, to share your fortune with him, an amount of some $46,000 in gold

> and silver coins, $12,000 in jewelry and several gold watches. In return your son was to be helped to escape into Tennessee. Your son was not killed during the fighting, Harrington murdered him later on the pretext that he was escaping. With my help, Harrington removed the cache and hid it in a saltpeter cave, about a quarter of a mile distant from the little town church. Harrington was accidentally killed in a blast while we were destroying the saltpeter caves before we abandoned the area. I took a minie ball at the Battle of Seven Mile Ford and have been unable to travel since. I had planned to return to Saltville and reveal the location of your money to you. But I am dying and I want you to know that I took no part in the murder of your son. Respectfully, Corporal Allen E.Brooks, late of the Fortieth Mounted Infantry, Army of the U.S., General Stoneman Commanding

Using the letter from Corporal Brooks as a guide, Samuel Smith tried several times to find the treasure. The saltpeter cave was a natural cave in Poor Valley, between Allison's Gap and Saltville. Many caves in the area had been blasted shut and otherwise destroyed by Stoneman's troops during the battle of the salt works, and removing the debris from all of them would have been a formidable and expensive task for Samuel Smith. His efforts to find the treasure proved vain, and he eventually gave up and moved away.

Most who have researched this tale believe that the Smith treasure is hidden in a cavern known locally as Harmon's Cave. All attempts at finding the fifty-eight thousand dollars' worth of gold and silver coins and jewels, however, have failed. There are several other caves in this region, and in one of them, it is likely that the Smith fortune still reposes on the floor of some deep chamber.

The Gray Ghost's Lost Treasure

General John Singleton Mosby was one of the better known and more colorful leaders of the Confederate army during the War Between The States. A University of Virginia graduate and practicing lawyer, Mosby joined the Southern army as a private at the outbreak of the war. After serving as scout for General J.E.B. Stuart during the Peninsula Campaign and earning recognition for valor at Bull Run and Antietam, Mosby was promoted to colonel. In 1863, he organized and led a guerrilla unit called Mosby's Raiders. With this team of fearless fighting men, he conducted a campaign of harassment and predation against Union forces in Virginia and Maryland that made his name legendary. Union soldiers, who had no success in pursuing Mosby and his raiders, began calling him the "Gray Ghost," a name by which he is still known.

In the spring of 1863, Mosby captured three hundred fifty thousand dollars' worth of gold, silver, jewelry, and coins during a desperate flight from Yankee pursuit and buried it secretly in Fauquier County in the Appalachian Piedmont.

Mosby and his raiders had attacked the Fairfax courthouse, where they surprised and captured Union General Edwin H. Stoughton. Though a general, Stoughton was never seen as much of a leader by most Union officers. The overweight and overbearing general had too much appetite for fine foods, wines, and women, and he lacked enthusiasm for combat. When Colonel Mosby and his hand-picked guerrillas entered the courthouse, they found Stoughton surrounded by casks of wine and great stores of food. Stoughton had apparently taken over the courthouse as his private quarters for the duration of the war, and in spite of the bloody conflict around him, the hedonistic general saw to it that he himself wanted for little during those trying times.

Though Stoughton was guarded by two captains and thirty-eight enlisted men, the practiced raiders took him with ease. Mosby also captured fifty-eight horses, several carriages, numerous crates of victuals and drink, and about three hundred fifty thousand dollars' worth of gold and silver plate, coins, jewelry, and tableware that Stoughton's soldiers had looted from Southern homes. Colonel Mosby had all the valuables gathered up and placed in a large canvas bag.

Learning that large Union forces were in the area searching for him, Mosby had his guerrillas hurriedly load the booty into the carriages, and with Stoughton and his men as prisoners, they fled southwest toward the town of Culpeper, where General Stuart awaited them.

Mosby's Raiders, along with the captives and cargo, raced through the rolling hills of the Appalachian Piedmont, a low eroded plateau that offered a transition from the rugged highlands to gentle lay of the coastal plain.

When the guerrilla force crossed into Fauquier County, one of Mosby's scouts raced back to the colonel with the news that a Union cavalry contingent was bearing down on them from the northeast. Because the captured goods were slowing the retreat to Culpeper, Mosby decided to ditch the barrels of wine and the crates of food. He also elected to bury the large canvas sack of treasure.

By Mosby's later recollection, the raiders halted briefly about midway between the towns of Haymarket and New Baltimore to unload the excess baggage. While his soldiers quickly dumped the cargo from the carriages, Mosby, accompanied by his trusted sergeant James F. Ames, carried the large sack some distance from the trail and placed it in a hastily dug hole between two tall pine trees. After filling the hole, Mosby notched several tree trunks with his knife so the site could be easily identified on a return visit.

Mosby expected to retrace his trail within a few days and dig up the treasure, but the war kept him busy and carried him farther and farther from Fauquier County.

When the war was over, Mosby returned to his law practice and settled in western Virginia, far from where he fought during the war. He never returned to the piedmont to retrieve the treasure.

Mosby, as well as members of his crack guerrilla unit, often told of burying the treasure along the rocky trail during the flight from the Fairfax courthouse. Though many knew about the fortune, only Mosby and Ames knew the exact location. Sergeant Ames, however, would never reveal the secret. During the war, he was captured by General George Armstrong Custer and hanged at Fort Royal.

When asked why he never returned for the treasure, John S. Mosby, the famed Gray Ghost and Confederate War hero, would always evade the question and change the subject.

Of course, the question of the buried treasure would return. It was raised again in 1916 when Mosby was eighty-three and near death. Responded the Gray Ghost,

> I've always meant to return to the area and look for that cache we buried after capturing Stoughton. Some of the most precious heirlooms of old Virginia were buried there. I guess that one of these days someone will find it.

The cached canvas sack of gold, silver, jewelry, and other items hidden by Mosby on that spring day in 1863 would be worth several million dollars today. Many treasure hunters have tried to retrace Mosby's retreat from the Fairfax courthouse to the rendezvous with General Stuart at Culpeper, but none could ever be certain of the route.

The Snow Hill Farm Treasure

Sometime in the late 1760s, a Scotsman named William Kirk brought his wife to Fauquier County to settle. The couple was soft-spoken and rarely found in the company of others. Their reclusiveness was a small mystery to the townspeople of New Baltimore, who would have been shocked to learn of the notorious background of this polite, kindly, and well-dressed man.

Years earlier, William Kirk had been an infamous pirate. His years of freebooting brought him adventure and great wealth, but as he grew older, he realized his violent days at sea were numbered. By anyone's standard, Kirk was a wealthy man, made rich by looting the merchant vessels that plied the ocean between North America and Europe.

Taking his wealth, Kirk retired from pirating and lived quietly in a small town on the Carolina coast. Here he met and married his wife, and settled into respectability, determined to keep his lawless past a secret. In time, Kirk and his wife decided to move to the higher lands of the Virginia Piedmont. Through an intermediary, he arranged to buy Snow Hill Farm, a relatively prosperous plantation in Fauquier County about a mile south of the New Baltimore settlement. Kirk proved as adept at running a large farm as he had been at piracy. He hired several men to work on his plantation and soon turned it into a prosperous enterprise.

All the while, Kirk and his wife fed local curiosity about their lives by rarely going to town, preferring instead to send one of the hired men.

Kirk distrusted banks and hid his wealth in places known only to himself. The ex-buccaneer never told his wife about any of his secret caches. Afraid someone might accidentally discover one of them, he would occasionally dig them up and rebury them elsewhere. According to documents in the Fauquier County courthouse, Kirk possessed an estimated sixty thousand dollars in gold and silver coins, a tremendous fortune for the time.

Kirk and his wife apparently lived a quiet and happy life on Snow Hill Farm for about eighteen years. His health finally began to deteriorate from several serious bouts of pneumonia, and William Kirk died in his sleep in 1779. Before he did, he drafted a will leaving his entire estate to his wife. The will alerted her to the cached wealth. She searched for months after his death, but never found any of it.

Though she lived in relative comfort for many years, the work and responsibility of running Snow Hill Farm became too much for the Widow Kirk, and she eventually sold the property to a man named William Edmonds. Edmonds continued to farm the plantation much as Kirk had, and the property passed down through a succession of his heirs.

In the 1870s, the Edmonds descendants ran most of Snow Hill Farm on shares, paying several sharecroppers a part of the profits of their harvest and letting them live on the land. One day, one of the tenant farmers was breaking ground in a field when the plow hit something hard in the dirt. Thinking he had struck a rock, the farmer stopped the mule and went to work to remove it. His plow had hit a large porcelain crock. Removing the lid, the astonished farmer found the crock filled with gold and silver coins.

Not sure what to do with his find, he returned to his modest home and sent his youngest son to tell the plantation owner of the discovery. Between the time the lad was sent and the owner arrived, the farmer thought better of announcing his discovery and hid the crock, keeping only a handful of the coins in his pocket. When the owner arrived, the farmer showed him the few coins he had set aside. The plantation owner was unimpressed with the discovery and let the farmer keep the few coins.

A few weeks later, the landowner began to wonder what the sharecropper had actually found. It seems he purchased a nearby farm for eight thousand dollars in cash and spent another two thousand dollars on equipment and supplies.

Many New Baltimore residents of the time believed the sharecropper had chanced upon a cache from William Kirk's fortune, booty taken long ago in pirating escapades. The story of the discovery soon spread throughout the piedmont and people came to Snow Hill Farm to search the fields for other likely caches. Over the years, several coins minted in the eighteenth and nineteenth centuries have been found on the old plantation, but no large caches.

Some fifty thousand dollars of the original William Kirk pirate fortune could still be hidden somewhere on Snow Hill Farm, and if it were found, could well be worth ten to twenty times that amount today.

If the original boundaries of the Snow Hill Farm when it was purchased by Kirk in the 1760s could be determined, it would be easy to grid the property and systematically explore it with a sophisticated metal detector. Simple enough—if the present owners would permit it, and if the treasure has not already been discovered and removed.

The Doll House Treasure of Upshur County

From the Appalachian Plateau region of West Virginia comes one of the more bizarre tales of hidden treasure, a tale of a strange and reclusive Spaniard, an even stranger miniature house, and three hundred thirty thousand dollars of alleged bank robbery loot.

The Appalachian Plateau, which takes in most of northern and western West Virginia, is an elevated tract of nearly flat to gently folded land ranging in altitude from a thousand feet along the western edge to more than three thousand feet where it meets the Allegheny Front in the east and south. Ancient glacial abrasion and the more recent erosion by flowing water have sculpted the plateau into gentle hills and deep valleys.

Into one of these valleys in 1889 came a dark little stoop-shouldered man. Giving his name as Alfonso Marzo, the man approached a farmer named Shahan about purchasing some land on which to build a cabin. Marzo, who claimed he was from Spain, offered gold. Shahan and Marzo haggled briefly, then struck a deal, and the Spaniard became the owner of a few acres near the railroad tracks about a mile from Shahan's house.

Carrying all his possessions in a large canvas sack and a suitcase-sized metal trunk, Marzo moved onto his new property and built a house. It was a queer little home, a dramatically scaled-down version of a normal frame house that looked like a miniature such as one would build for young children to play in. The neighbors dubbed it the "doll house."

Though Shahan and other local residents tried to be friendly, Marzo remained distant. He shunned visitors and actually fled into the woods at the approach of strangers. Marzo rarely visited town to purchase supplies, and on the few times he did venture into a settlement, he conducted what little business he had and left as quickly as possible.

Marzo gave Shahan the impression that he was a blacksmith, but he didn't seem to have any of the tools of that trade. Other than building the doll house, Marzo was never seen to work.

Marzo lived on his property for nearly four years, then suddenly and mysteriously disappeared. The Spaniard left no word with anyone—he simply vanished. All that remained to remind anyone of him was the odd doll house, still seen occasionally by passers-by.

Several years elapsed, and Shahan was surprised to receive a letter one day from Marzo. It was dated August 17, 1911, and was postmarked Madrid, Spain. The letter read,

> My Dear Sir: I am imprisoned in this city and knowing your honesty and personality, I beg to beseech you to herewith whether you want to come here to take away my equipages seizure in order to seize upon a trunk containing a secret in which I have hidden a document indispensible to you to come in possession of 330,000 dollars that I have in the United States. As a reward, I will yield to you the third part of the aforementioned sum.
>
> Fearful that this letter don't arrive at your hands, I will want your answer and then I will say you my secret with every detail and to subscribe with my name.

As here is a newspaper that publish all the cablegrams whose addressee are unknown which it is allowed to me to read and I cannot receive here in the gaol your reply, you must send a cablegram to the address indicated at the end.

Notwithstanding, your cable not reach to me, this will be sufficient to know that you accept my proposition.

Waiting eagerly to read your missive.

I only inscribe
V. ex-banker

Above all, please answer by cable, but not by letter, as following:

Alfonso Marzo
Ysabel Catolica ZO- Madrid
Yes—Julius

While much of Marzo's letter is vague and difficult to interpret, probably a result of the Spaniard's poor command of the English language, some points are clear. First, Marzo apparently knew where three hundred thirty thousand dollars lay hidden and had secreted a document somewhere which gave directions to the cache. Was the trunk the letter mentioned the same one he brought to the West Virginia valley? Second, Marzo was apparently willing to share a third of the alleged wealth with Shahan. Third, the Spaniard said he was a prisoner in Madrid, although he gave no explanation.

Shahan had trouble understanding the cryptic letter and was not quite certain what to make of it. In any case, he did not reply to the Spaniard and never received any more correspondence from him.

One element of Marzo's mysterious letter has puzzled researchers for years: If the three hundred thousand dollars did, in fact, exist, where did it come from and how did it come to be in the Spaniard's possession?

Perhaps Marzo's fortune can be tied to an incident that occurred elsewhere in the state several weeks before his quiet arrival at the Shahan farm. Somewhere east of Upshur County, a bank was robbed, and the little documentation that exists suggests that about a third of a million dollars was taken. Coincidence?

And what of the doll house? No satisfactory reason has ever been given for the building of the strange little structure. Did it have anything to do with the three hundred thirty thousand dollars? A story told around Upshur County following the arrival of Marzo's letter was that the Spaniard had indeed robbed the bank and fled with his stolen loot to the Appalachian Plateau, where he buried it beneath the doll house.

This tale sent many area residents to the valley in which Marzo had lived, searching for the miniature house. They could never find it. Farmer Shahan, who seldom visited the Marzo property when the Spaniard was there, rode over shortly after receiving the letter. The doll house was gone. There was no evidence that it had fallen down or burned; it had simply disappeared without a trace. Try as they might, neither Shahan nor any of his neighbors could remember just where the mysterious doll house had sat on the property.

Attempts to trace Alfonso Marzo back to Spain failed, and what became of him remains a mystery. As far as anyone knows, the Spaniard never returned to the Appalachian Plateau to reclaim any of the treasure thought buried on his small plot of land.

Documents on the old Shahan farm locate it near the junction of Bear Camp Run and the left fork of the Buckhannon River in the southeastern corner of Upshur County. Somewhere not far from the original Shahan cabin, the mysterious doll house treasure still lies buried.

The Peddler's Lost Cache

Moishe Edelman was an unlikely source of buried treasure, but over the course of several years, the old immigrant peddler apparently buried several thousands of dollars' worth of gold coins in a secret location in West Virginia, intending someday to retrieve them. Edelman, however, suffered a fatal heart attack and died before he could enjoy any of the fruits of his hard work and systematic saving. Before he died, Edelman stammered out the directions to his buried fortune to the physician who was attending him in a Cleveland, Ohio, hospital.

Moishe Edelman, known to his customers as "Mose," was born early in the 1880s in a Jewish ghetto in Russia. As a boy, Moishe was weak and sickly and often complained of chest pains. In his teens, Moishe fled Russia and made his way to England, where he could not find decent work. The young man often labored eighteen hours a day at menial jobs that paid little, but because he was frugal, he saved enough money to buy a steamer ticket to the United States.

When Moishe arrived in America, he worked at various low-paying jobs and eventually became a peddler. In the beginning, the young man toted a large canvas sack filled with household wares such as were needed by the people of the remote and rural parts of the Appalachians in Virginia and West Virginia. Burdened by the heavy bag, the dedicated merchant traveled on foot from house to house and farm to farm, selling his goods. Travel was usually difficult in the rugged, sparsely settled Appalachians during that time, and the weather was often disagreeable, but Moishe persevered. Between 1916 and 1930, he walked thousands of miles of back-country roads in the hills and valleys of the Appalachian Plateau.

Because Moishe had miserly habits and no family or other apparent expenses, his savings grew. By 1930, he had amassed what in those days amounted to a large fortune. The immigrant peddler's distrust of banks led him to convert his money into gold coins and bury them on a riverbank somewhere in Lincoln County in western West Virginia.

As Moishe grew older, carrying a heavy pack through the rugged mountain country exacted an increasingly heavy toll on his frail frame. He finally bought an inexpensive secondhand automobile. Moishe occasionally would stay in a hotel, but more often than not, he lived in his old car.

In June 1933, Moishe drove to Ohio to purchase a new line of household goods from a dealer he knew. While loading merchandise into his car, the peddler was felled by a sudden heart attack and rushed to the local hospital. After several days of intensive care and many consultations with the attending physician, Moishe realized that his weakened heart would not recover and that he would soon die.

One morning when the doctor stopped by Moishe's room, the peddler reached out and grasped the physician's lab coat and pulled him closer. Feeling weaker with each passing moment, the dying man haltingly whispered to the doctor that he had something important he needed to tell him. With difficulty, Moishe told him how he had acquired wealth and then buried gold coins many times along a remote creek bank in West Virginia. When he told the doctor he wished to give him directions to the fortune, the physician grabbed a notepad and pencil and quickly jotted down the peddler's final words:

> Go along the hard road until you reach Fry, a small community between Logan and Huntington, West Virginia. Go toward the settlement of Leet across the mountain from Fry. At Leet, Laurel Fork Creek empties into the Big Ugly River. Go up Laurel Fork for a mile or two until you reach a large rock. Directly across the road from the rock, in a small bend of the creek, thousands of dollars are in four chests. Dig along the bank.

A few moments later, Moishe Edelman, peddler, was dead.

The doctor believed Edelman was sincere, and that the information he gave was not a raving caused by delerium.

Several weeks later, the doctor took several days off to travel to Lincoln County, West Virginia, where he searched for Moishe Edelman's buried treasure. The physician was amazed to discover how remote and rugged the area was, and how many miles of creek bank might conceal the peddler's gold coins. Several spots along Laurel Fork Creek fit Edelman's description, but after digging a series of holes at several sites, the doctor came away with nothing. Discouraged by his poor luck and the immensity of the task, and burdened by the obligations of his medical practice, the physician packed up and returned to Cleveland after a few days.

Moishe Edelman's description does include a lot of territory. Perhaps someday a treasure hunter with a reliable metal detector and a bit of luck may uncover the old peddler's buried money.

Hidden Treasure in the Buckhannon River Valley

During the height of the Civil War, a soldier whose name has been lost to history dropped by the Wilson farm in a sparsely settled portion of Monongalia County. The soldier and Wilson were old friends, and the farmer and his wife asked their guest to stay the night.

Wondering why his friend was not with his military unit, Wilson asked several pointed questions. The soldier said he was on temporary leave, and then unfolded an amazing tale of a hidden treasure for which he was searching. The vast fortune lay in a lost cave in the upper reaches of the Buckhannon River Valley, about fifty miles to the south in Upshur County.

The soldier had just returned from Upshur County where he had been thwarted in his search by roving bands of outlaws and opposing military detachments, both making travel through the remote and unprotected West Virginia wilderness difficult, if not impossible.

After the evening meal, when the soldier and Wilson were alone, the guest opened a large leather traveling bag and took out an eighteen-inch-square parchment map. He showed Wilson where the map said the treasure was buried. The soldier told Wilson about a party of miners who had been taking bags of coins and ingots of silver east when they were set upon by a roving band of Indians. Fleeing, the miners hid in a cave and buried the ingots and coins in the far corner of a large chamber. In the dark of night, the miners silently crept from their hiding place and continued their journey east, intending to come back someday for the fortune. The miners, according to the young soldier, never returned and the treasure still lay in the cave. His map was made by one of the miners, who drowned in a rain-swollen river while trying to return to the cave.

The map, he said, was useless without its key, held by a close friend just to the west, in Marion County.

Wilson shared the soldier's enthusiasm for the hidden treasure. The two agreed to become partners, get the key, and search for the treasure together. The soldier, however, was overdue in reporting back to his cavalry unit and said that he needed to be on his way. Leaving the map with Wilson, the soldier gave directions to the Marion County resident with the map key. He asked Wilson to wait for him to return, but to pursue the search on his own if he was not back within a reasonable time after the war ended. With that, the soldier bid farewell to his friend and rode away into the woods. The farmer never saw him again.

Wilson waited nearly two years after the end of the war for his partner's return. Finally, he decided to go to Marion County and get the key. Wilson packed a wagon, hitched up two stout horses, and at the last minute, invited his grandson along. The trip through the rugged and often dangerous wilderness was long and hard, an unforgettable experience for the younger Wilson.

Decades later, when Joseph M. Wilson was himself a grandfather, he easily recalled the arduous trip through the Appalachian backcountry. It rained often and they had difficulty crossing streams. The wagon occasionally bogged down in the mud and the two had to slog through muck and high water to help the horses pull free. The younger Wilson also recalled that at one point during the return trip, his grandfather told him he now had the key and could go directly to the cave and find the treasure. Unfortunately, once they returned home, the old man became very sick and died.

Because he was so young, Joseph Wilson had little inkling of the potential worth of the buried treasure that the map and key supposedly led to. Several years later, when he had developed an appreciation for the value of money, he recalled his grandfather's quest. He also recalled that his grandfather was a very conservative man, not one to waste time. That he had traveled across two counties to get the key to the treasure map suggested to young Wilson that the old man had thought it important.

Joseph Wilson's family moved to another valley, but when he was old enough, he went to his grandmother's home and asked about the map and the key left by his late grandfather. After searching through several drawers, old trunks, and bundles of papers, he found the map. Carefully unrolling it, young Wilson noted that it was a very old, stiff parchment. The inscriptions on the map were finely written in ink, and while clear and easy to read, were vague about the amount and type of treasure. Nothing on the map told the origin of the treasure or who buried it.

Diligent searching failed to turn up the key. The grandmother, who could neither read nor write, confessed she might have burned it along with some other papers she considered worthless.

After several weeks of studying the map, the younger Wilson determined that the treasure had long ago been hidden in a cave close to the old Seneca War Trail where it crossed the upper Buckhannon River in Upshur County. According to the map, the trail could be seen from the cave's low entrance.

Without the key, Joseph Wilson searched for the treasure cave several times but never found it. After several years, he gave up, and in 1891 turned the map over to one Lucullus Virgil McWhorter, a native of the town of Buckhannon. McWhorter was one of the few educated men living in the area at the time. During the early 1880s, McWhorter had conducted a detailed study of local Indian artifacts and campgrounds. Wilson gave McWhorter the map because he seemed keenly interested in local history.

Wilson also told McWhorter what he knew of the origin of the map, and of the lost key. McWhorter was interested in the tale of buried treasure and tried to find it several times himself, with no success. In 1915, McWhorter published an account of the lost treasure cave.

Though many others, using the old parchment map or copies of it, have searched for the lost treasure cave, none have found it. Researchers have diligently pursued an explanation for the origin of the treasure, and many believe that it is part of a shipment of silver ingots from one of the famed Jonathan Swift mines. *(See "The Lost Jonathan Swift Mines," page 76.)*

Members of the Swift party often passed through the Buckhannon River Valley on their way to and from the mines in Kentucky, and Jonathan Swift himself makes several references to the area in his journals. One particular entry by Swift may shed some light on the hidden treasure.

While establishing a temporary camp along what many think was the Buckhannon River, the Swift party was suddenly attacked by Indians. Quickly strapping the packs of ingots and equipment onto their mules, the miners fled along the Seneca Trail, eventually taking refuge in a cave near the headwaters of the stream. While several men guarded the entrance, others buried the bars of silver. Relieved of their heavy load, the miners waited until darkness and then escaped, intending someday to return and retrieve the wealth secreted in some dark chamber of the cave.

It may also be worth noting that Swift occasionally referred to rich silver mines in the Buckhannon River Valley which he and his men excavated during 1761. It may very well have been silver taken from one of these mines that was cached in the lost cave.

Many mining tools, all of the them quite old, have been found in the Buckhannon River Valley, and they may have belonged to the Swift party. In addition, at least two very old mine shafts have been discovered. The shafts had been covered up in a careless attempt at concealment, but years of erosion have exposed the openings.

Few people these days have reason to travel to the relatively isolated upper reaches of the Buckhannon River in Upshur County. The local tales and legends of lost mines and buried treasures are relatively unknown to outsiders, and so there have been few organized attempts to find the lost cave. Continued research and organized, systematic exploration of the area might someday yield one of the country's largest treasure caches.

Other Tales of Lost and Buried Treasures in West Virginia

Cavern of Gold by Bear Fork Creek

Two friends were deer hunting near Bear Fork Creek in Gilmer County in the early 1950s when they accidentally discovered a thick seam of gold in a remote cavern.

The two had taken a few days off from their jobs as coal miners. Happy to be away from the mines and out in the peace and solitude of the forest, the friends approached the hunt with enthusiasm. Around mid-morning of their second day in the woods, they had spotted fresh deer tracks and followed them for nearly two miles when they chanced upon a cave.

Neither of the men had ever been in a cave, and they decided to explore this one. Carrying crude torches made from grasses and tree limbs, the two crept cautiously into the dark passageway. Sixty yards into the cave, they noticed one wall painted with Indian signs and symbols. While one examined the markings, the other discovered a long, thick line of color transecting the opposite wall. On closer inspection, the hunters discovered the color was a vein of gold.

The two friends returned to their homes and jobs the following day and began to make plans to return to the cave to excavate some of the rich ore. Several months passed before they could coordinate their vacation time so they could go back to Gilmer County, find the cave again, and dig out some of the gold.

Eventually they returned to Bear Fork Creek, where they set up camp. On the morning of the following day, the two friends began their search. Armed with digging tools, they trudged up and down hills and through valleys, trying to retrace the route they had followed tracking the deer months earlier. After three days of fruitless searching, they admitted they had no inkling where the cave might be. They had failed to take note of pertinent landmarks and features in their haste to get home after their discovery. The two men thought they could walk right to the cave of gold, but in the several months since their trip, they had apparently forgotten much of what they saw. Disheartened, they returned home.

Apparently known to the Indians of long ago, the cave of gold remains lost.

Hidden Gold in Jefferson County

Colonel Joseph Van Swearingen, a retired veteran of the Revolutionary War, bought a small farm and settled into the community of Bellevue in Jefferson County. Swearingen had been a soldier for nearly forty years and had grown weary of the profession. He looked forward to living out the rest of his life in leisure, growing a few crops on the acreage he purchased.

During his years in the military, Swearingen had accumulated impressive wealth, much of it booty he had taken in wartime. Though no one knew exactly how much money the old soldier had, the Bellevue townsfolk saw the colonel as an extremely wealthy man.

One day while in a nearby town on business, Swearingen visited a fortune teller who predicted he would die within the year. Normally not one to believe in such things, Swearingen began to think of his mortality, and decided to hide his fortune. Somewhere on his farm, Swearingen had a field hand dig a pit, and into the pit he put an iron kettle filled with gold and silver coins. He told no one where it was buried, and as far as anyone knows, left no written record of it either.

Within the year, Swearingen died—at the exact hour and day predicted by the spiritualist. Swearingen left no heirs, and the small farm soon fell into disrepair. Stories of his buried wealth spread throughout the area, and occasional treasure hunters would set up camp for a few days at the old farm while they searched for the buried coins. The cache was never recorded as having been found.

The Lost Fort Seybert Treasure

Old Fort Seybert lay in the heart of Indian country, and relationships between the fort's inhabitants and the Shawnee were strained at best. In 1758, growing tensions gave way to violence, and the Shawnee launched a vicious attack on the fort, killing most of the soldiers and capturing many civilians living in the stockade. The Shawnee decided to keep the white prisoners as slaves and roped them together and marched them from the fort toward the Indian village several miles away.

Before leaving the fort, the Indians had the settlers gather up all their valuables and put them in a large iron kettle. When the kettle was filled, the Indians inserted a wooden pole through the handle and had two of the male captives carry it to the Shawnee village. The big pot full of gold and silver coins and other valuables was heavy and hard to manage. The two men assigned to it wrestled with the cumbersome load, sometimes falling and spilling the contents.

To reach the Shawnee village, the party of Indians and captives followed a well-used trail up one side of South Fork Mountain. As the trail grew steeper, the men carrying the treasure-filled kettle had even greater difficulty. Finally, the Shawnee chief, tired of the clumsiness of the white men, ordered them to leave the pot and signaled the group to continue the march. When the column was out of sight, the chief had two of his braves scrape out a hole and bury the pot and its contents. This was done in a few minutes, and the Indians rejoined the group and continued on to the village.

Several weeks later, the Shawnee village was attacked by a large rescue party. The Indians were routed and the captives returned to safety. After their release, several of the former prisoners tried to find the pot of coins, but saw no evidence of a recent excavation. Since the Shawnee were driven from the area never to return, they probably didn't have a chance to retrieve the treasure.

If the route from Fort Seybert to the Shawnee village could be retraced, a persistent and fortunate treasure hunter with a good metal detector might find the buried kettle of coins.

Abandoned Union Payroll Near Chapmanville

In Fayette County during the War Between The States, a contingent of Union soldiers was escorting a large payroll—a wagon full of gold coins—to a Yankee encampment in the area. As the party traveled along the winding trails through the dense woods, scouts told the commanding officer that a Confederate patrol was rapidly approaching from the east.

The Union officer ordered the escort into a full gallop in the hope of outdistancing the Rebels, but after trying to elude the enemy for about five miles, it became clear that they would soon be overtaken. Anticipating a skirmish, the officer halted the wagon and ordered the canvas bags that held the Union payroll taken from the wagon and buried a short distance from the trail. While troopers hastily dug a pit in which to hide the gold, the officer noted the surroundings in his journal. He wrote that the payroll was hidden on the west side of the Buyandotte River, near a small settlement named Chapmanville.

Once the hole was filled, the soldiers remounted and rode on. About an hour later, the Confederates overtook the Union soldiers and opened fire. The Yankees sought cover and returned fire, but they were disorganized and greatly outnumbered. The fighting lasted about two hours, and when it was over, all of the Yankee soldiers lay dead.

The Rebel soldiers searched the wagon for the money and found it empty. Suspecting the gold had been buried shortly before the engagement, they retraced the Yankees' trail for several miles, without finding the payroll.

Returning to the site of the skirmish, the Confederates stripped the Union soldiers of anything of value and left the corpses to rot in the sun. An unknown soldier took the commanding officer's journal and later tossed it into a trunk and forgot it. In the early 1930s, someone discovered the old journal and searched unsuccessfully for the buried coins.

The directions in the journal claimed the gold was buried at a point where the old road and the Buyandotte River came within twenty yards of one another. Since the war, however, the road has been all but obliterated by a more modern thoroughfare, and the river has shifted its course.

If the Union payroll of gold coins was not uncovered by the shifting river and washed downstream, the Civil War cache is probably still lying just a few inches beneath the soil near Chapmanville.

References

Anderson, Nina and Bill Andrews. *Southern Treasures*. Chester, Connecticut: The Globe Pequot Press, 1987.

Andrews, Ernest M. *Georgia's Fabulous Treasure Hoards*. Hapeville, Georgia: E.M. Andrews, 1966.

Atchley, D. Van. "West Virginia's Lost Gold Mine." *Western And Eastern Treasures* (December 1978): 50.

Bailey, Jay. "John Swift's Lost Silver Mines—Fact or Fiction." *True Treasure* (January-February 1970): 58-64.

Belcher, D.R. and Wade Chastain. "New Clues To The Carolinas' Incredible Spanish Treasure." *Treasure Search* (April 1983): 6-10.

Boren, Kerry Ross. "Lost Silver Crowns Of The Appalachians." *True Treasure* (November-December 1972): 28-33.

________. "Lost Mines And Buried Treasures In The Trans-Allegheny." *Treasure World* (June-July 1975): 11-13.

Bradley, Bob. "Civil War Loot In Tennessee." *Lost Treasure* (June 1978): 50.

Brown, Dee. "Legends of Confederate Gold." *Southern Magazine* (November 1987): 49-51, 88-90.

Clark, Jafar. "Confederate Gold In North Carolina." *Lost Treasure* (March 1978): 61-62.

Dangerfield, Dan. "Where Are The Melungeon Mines?" *Lost Treasure* (October 1978): 28-29, 49-50.

Duffy, Howard M. "Snow Hill Pirate Trove." *Lost Treasure* (November 1976): 31.

________. "Confederate Treasure." *Lost Treasure* (May 1977): 45-46.

Everman, William J. "Lekain's Lost Silver Cache." *True Treasure* (October 1974): 40-41, 48-50, 52.

Harris, Charles S. "The Civil War Treasure Of Tasso, Tennessee." *Treasure Search* (Summer 1973) 32-35.

Harvey, Davis E. "Lost Alabama Silver." *Lost Treasure* (December 1976): 23-24.

________. "Georgia's $250,000 Treasure Tunnel." *Western And Eastern Treasures* (October 1977): 24-25.

Henson, Michael Paul. "West Virginia Treasure Cave." *Treasure Search* (March 1975): 54-55.

________. "Kentucky's Five Barrels Of Silver." *Treasure* (May 1975): 68-69.

________. "Lost Silver Mine In West Virginia." *True Treasure* (September-October 1975): 13-15.

________. *A Guide To Treasure In Virginia And West Virginia*. Deming, New Mexico: Carson Enterprises, 1982.

________. *A Guide To Treasure In Kentucky*. Deming, New Mexico: Carson Enterprises, 1984.

________. "$330,000 West Virginia Cache." *Treasure* (October 1986): 24, 59.

________. "Clues To The Swift Silver Mines." *Treasure* (December 1987): 24, 51.

________. "West Virginia Treasures." *Lost Treasure* (February 1980): 8-14.

Hudson, C.M. "Drowned Man's Gold." *Lost Treasure* (July 1978): 36.

Hughes, Brent. "Find The Cave—Find The Gold!" *Lost Treasure* (May 1988): 20-22.

Hunt, Burl. "Crismo's Captured Coins." *Lost Treasure* (June 1979): 57-58.

Hunt, Charles B. *Natural Regions Of The United States And Canada*. San Francisco: W.H. Freeman and Co., 1974.

Malach, Roman. "Bone Cave Gold." *Treasure Search* (June 1985): 18.

________. "Lekain's Coins." *Treasure* (January 1986): 28, 74.

Masters, Al. "Treasure In West Virginia." *Treasure World* (November 1975): 25.

________. "Multi-Million Dollar Treasure Of Red Bone Cave." *Lost Treasure* (September 1979): 27-29.

Milberger, Joe F. "Bellfaun's Gold In A Pot Of Clay." *Western And Eastern Treasures* (May 1977): 42-44.

Raitz, Karl B. and Richard Ulack. *Appalachia: A Regional Geography*. Boulder, Colorado: Westview Press, 1984.

Ronoto. "The Doll House Treasure In West Virginia." *Western And Eastern Treasures* (February 1979): 18-20.

Rush, J.William. "Find Bechtler's Lost Carolina Fortunes." *Treasure* (January 1979): 56-59, 61.

Steely, Michael S. "Silver Arrowhead Points To Legendary Swift's Mines." *Treasure* (September, 1984): 8-10.

Townsend, Tom. "Lost Gold Of The Uwharries." *Lost Treasure* (November, 1976): 55-56.

Traywick, Ben T. "Mystery Silver Mine." *Lost Treasure* (February 1988): 16-18.

Van Dyke, R.E. "Elkhead Hoard." *Treasure* (October, 1985): 51-52.

Wade, Forest C. *Cry Of The Eagle: History And Legends Of The Cherokee Indians And Their Buried Treasures*. Cumming, Georgia: F.C. Wade, 1969.

Ward, John K. "Dix River's Buried Bandit Loot." *Lost Treasure* (October, 1977): 33-36.

Weber, Glenn. "Missing $115,000 In Confederate Gold." *Treasure World* (June-July 1973): 29.

Williams, Jerry. "Asa Smyth's Keg Of Gold." *Treasure Search* (April, 1985): 48-49.

Other books of interest from
August House Publishers